I0687514

Just for You

by

Kay Harris

I Want Morrison, Book Three

Just for You

Contact Information: info@thewildrosepress.com

Cover Art by *Kristian Norris*

The Wild Rose Press, Inc.
PO Box 708
Adams Basin, NY 14410-0708
Visit us at www.thewildrosepress.com

Publishing History
First Champagne Rose Edition, 2018
Print ISBN 978-1-5092-2153-0
Digital ISBN 978-1-5092-2154-7

I Want Morrison, Book Three
Published in the United States of America

"Look, just call him for a reference. When you get it and it's excellent—which it will be—can I have the job or not?"

"Why don't you just go back to Rick?"

She rolled her eyes and put a hand on her hip. "Because he'll want a multi-year commitment. And I'm only doing this for as long as it takes to get the money I need. And you are my best friend's brother-in-law, so I'm asking for a favor here."

I was a little surprised she willingly admitted she was asking for a favor. And I was about to revel in the reality that she may, in fact, be halfway human.

But then she ruined it. "Besides, you clearly need me. You're a complete disaster. I can start on Monday." Meg held out her hand as if for me to shake it.

I stared down at her tiny palm in the dim light. It waited, soft and elegant with intricately painted fingernails, to accept my own. "But you hate me," I pointed out.

"Don't remind me, rich boy. But I'm willing to overlook it. Do we have a deal or not?"

Perhaps it was the stench of the Dumpsters and my desire to be away from them, maybe it was the crisp night air affecting my thinking, or it could have been her beautiful form outlined in the evening light. But I shook her hand.

Dedication

To Stephanie, who encouraged me to write my first novel. I owe you for the writer I've become.

Chapter 1

Hayden
Present Day

I stare at the man in front of me. He smiles and beckons me to follow.

I take a step closer. "What are you doing here?"

He chuckles. "It's a long story. Come on," he says again.

With a shrug, I follow my brother-in-law through the black curtain and into a dimly lit backstage area. Without any further explanation, Henry meanders through a series of tables and chairs, past cardboard boxes bursting with linens, postcards, and God knows what else.

Occasionally, Henry glances back to make sure I'm following him. Eventually, after what seems like a long and convoluted journey, he opens a door and ushers me into a tiny room. It was clearly once a closet, and it is only large enough for one small round table with four folding chairs perched around it.

Sitting at the table, sipping on a can of soda, is a legendary rock star. And even though I've met the man before, I still have a moment. My breath hitches, and my brain tries to stall out.

"Hayden, good to see you, man," Hank Tolk says to me.

I nod weakly.

Henry slaps me on the back. "I found him wandering around out there." He sits at the chair closest to Hank and gestures for me to sit, too. I somehow manage to pull the chair away from the table and plop down in it. "So, what you doing here?" he asks me again.

I turn to Henry. "I come to the Fitness Festival every year. If I'd known you were into it, too, I would have invited you." I smirk a little with that comment. Henry is in good shape, but we both know he isn't a workout freak, like me.

"Hell no," Henry says, waving his hand at me. "I only came because my uncle got roped into being the special guest entertainment."

I turn to look at Henry's uncle. "So, you're the secret act they've been billing."

Hank Tolk shrugs one of his massive shoulders.

"Are you going to play?" I ask him, seeing no guitar anywhere in sight.

"Yeah, a couple of songs."

It makes sense really. Hank's muscular build is certainly the product of an intensive regime, and having him as the special guest entertainer for the last night of this conference for fitness geeks seems appropriate.

"I could have sworn I saw you with a woman when I first spotted you out there," Henry says, reaching into a cooler in the corner and pulling out a can of soda. He slides it across the table to me.

"I came with a date," I admit, listening to the crisp pop when I open the can.

"Hayden has been on the search for a wife," Henry tells his uncle. "He even has a matchmaker."

My stomach clenches at the mention of her. "Yeah."

"So, things are going well?"

I shake my head. "No. Actually, they're shit. Utter shit."

Hank Tolk leans forward in his seat. "Why's that?"

"The woman I brought, she's not… she's not really my date. She's a nice girl, and she knows exactly how fucked up my love life is. She came here with me as a friend."

Henry scrunches up his brow. "I don't get it. I mean, Chelsea said you were having a lot of dates, but she didn't think any of them went anywhere. So… frustrating, yeah, but fucked up?"

My sister has no idea what's really been going on, no one does.

"Forget the dates. All of them. They mean nothing. I'm in deep with a woman…" I look up at him. I like my brother-in-law, but I'm not sure he's the first person I would have called to spill my guts to. Nevertheless, he's here now, and I'm still reeling from having my heart crushed by a semi truck this morning. "I'm…I could probably stand to talk about it," I admit.

"I think so," Hank says. "We've got a couple of hours to kill. Why don't you tell us all about it?"

I look up at him. Telling my pathetic story to a legendary rock star had not exactly been on the agenda. Hell, none of this was.

"You sure?" I ask. "Don't you want to go out there and experience the conference?"

Hank waves his hand dismissively. "No way. I'm so not interested in walking around signing autographs. That's why I'm back here hiding, and I made Henry come along to keep me company." He leans back in his chair and takes a sip from his can. "So, tell us what's up. We can try to fix your love life."

"He's actually pretty good at it." Henry points his thumb over his shoulder at Hank. "He fixed my aunt and uncle when they broke up. That was like a quarter of century ago, and they're still together."

Hank reaches out with his long arm and smacks Henry on the back of the head. "Really? A quarter of a century? You gotta put it like that?" He shakes his head. "Punk." Then he looks up at me, his blue eyes piercing me. "Seriously, though. I lost my own girl once. And I had to figure out my shit to get her back. It helped to talk it through." He curls his fingers toward himself. "So. Out with it, Hayden."

"Um…okay…" I take a deep breath and spill.

****

Three months ago

"I love you, Hayden. I really do. But you're a disaster," Chelsea told me, after planting a kiss on my cheek.

"How late am I?" I asked, still out of breath from the rush to get there.

"Very. We're all done with the rehearsal," my sister's fiancé told me. "But on the bright side, you made it in time for dinner."

"I think he did it on purpose." Jack gave me a one-arm big-brother hug as he walked up behind me.

"Who the hell has a wedding rehearsal a week before the wedding?" I complained.

"We told you, it was the only time we could get—not the point," Chelsea said. "It's been on your calendar for months." She took my arm and walked me into the dining room of the resort.

The place was magnificent. I had to hand it to her and Henry. It was going to be a hell of a wedding, beautiful and intimate. The dining room, which was the same one the reception would be held in next Saturday, was a regally appointed affair fit for a modest group of eighty to one hundred people.

Tonight, however, we were only taking up three long tables near the rear of the room, by the floor-to-ceiling windows that overlooked the bay. Everyone else was already here and seated. As I walked toward the tables, I recognized my soon-to-be in-laws as well as my own family, nestled in and started on salad plates. Only four seats sat empty.

I watched as Chelsea and Henry took two seats side by side in the center of the middle table. Jack sat beside his wife at the table to the right and gestured to me to take the empty seat across from him. Jack's beautiful wife, Candace, smiled at me. When I managed to drag my gaze away from my sister-in-law, I looked at the people on either of side of the chair I was pulling out to sit in.

To my left sat Henry's sister, Gloria, who seemed like a nice enough gal, though I'd only met her once before. She was talking animatedly to Chelsea's friend, Tom. To my right sat Meg.

Shit.

I plopped down in the seat feeling defeated. I wondered how long and painful this meal would be. Not only did I have to watch my brother stare longingly at his wife across the table, I also had to sit next to her heinous friend who hated me.

"Nice of you to join us, rich boy," Meg cooed.

She'd been calling me that since I first met her. I rolled my eyes and avoided her gaze.

"Hayden, where have you been?" Candace asked me. She shifted my niece on her lap and leaned over the table toward me, causing her blouse to show way too much of her perfect cleavage.

I kept my eyes firmly on my plate as I answered. "My secretary quit yesterday."

My big brother groaned. "Please tell me you didn't sleep with her."

"That is so unfair," I said, looking up at him.

He pursed his lips, like he didn't believe me. "Then why did she quit?"

I sighed. "It turns out she was sleeping with Kent. And he dumped her and she got mad and left the company."

"Why would anyone sleep with Kent?" Candace asked, making a face.

"Yeah, that's disgusting," Jack agreed.

"I have a more important question."

The deep, crackly voice of the woman beside me forced me to turn toward her. A dangerous gleam sparkled in her brown eyes. "Oh God, let's hear it," I said sarcastically.

"Why the hell do you need a secretary to get to your sister's wedding rehearsal on time?" Meg asked.

"He's a brilliant man in many ways, Meg," Candace told her. "But he's not capable of actually scheduling his life. *That's* what he needs a secretary for."

Meg was truly a pain in my ass. But she was also indisputably gorgeous. Candace had told me once that Meg's mother was a native Hawaiian. That gene pool explained her dark complexion, round face, incredible chocolate eyes, and the most luscious curvy body I'd ever seen.

Her pretty face went from smirky to pensive to excited in the space of thirty seconds flat. I furrowed my brow at her. But she turned away and started eating her salad. I did the same.

I was starving. I had been in my home gym after working all day on a Saturday, when I got the frantic phone call from Jack wanting to know why I wasn't at the rehearsal yet. I'd been sweaty as hell and took the shortest shower in the history of forever before throwing on clothes and bolting over the Golden Gate to the North Bay.

I inhaled the mixed greens with a generous helping of dressing, then settled back to wait for the main course. Jack ribbed me, as he always did, about my healthy appetite. But the truth was, I had a pretty intense daily workout routine, and I burned every one of those calories.

While I was ignoring Jack and trying to be patient, my mother came over to give me a hard time about missing the rehearsal. Luckily, Candace had passed over my niece, Sandra, and she was nestled in my arms. The sight of her granddaughter peering up at her, sucking on her fingers as her wide eyes took in her surroundings, wiped the sour look off my mom's face and forced her to use a softer tone.

"Hayden, how are you going to know what to do next week during the real wedding?" my mom asked.

My mother was a loving woman. But she was also very concerned with appearances, which explained why she was always absolutely sculpted to perfection. From her dyed hair to her perfect makeup and collagen-enhanced lips, to her designer outfits, my mom fit into a high society none of her children were ever comfortable in.

"I'm an usher, Mom. It's not hard. Besides, Jack and I are doing it together. He will show me the ropes. I think we're good," I reassured her.

My mother left, still pissed at me. I was occasionally a major disappointment to her, but rather than ever saying that aloud, she just got mad. Just like when we were children, my brother thought that me being in trouble with Mom was hilarious and proceeded to give me a hard time through the rest of the meal.

After dinner and before dessert, I escaped to the men's room. As I emerged from the swinging door into the hallway, contemplating if I could get away with leaving this shindig early or not, I nearly ran over Meg. She stood in my path like a roadblock, her feet spread apart and her arms splayed out at her sides.

"What the hell?" I asked, coming to a screeching halt in front of her.

"We need to talk, rich boy." She pulled my arm and dragged me in the opposite direction to the dining room.

She pushed me through an exit door at the end of the hallway and out into the night air. It was dark and humid. A set of stinking Dumpsters stood nearby, and we perched at the top of a set of metal steps.

"What is this? A drug deal?" I asked, as I stumbled on the grated steps in my expensive shoes.

"I have to talk to you," she said again, standing right in front of me in the dark.

My eyes adjusted in time to see her face reflecting

enthusiasm. But I was at a complete loss as to why. "What on earth could you and I possibly have to talk about?"

"A job."

"A what?" I felt like I was in some bizarre dream. "A job?"

"Yes." She nodded her head vigorously. Her long, dark, impossibly straight hair flowed like rivers around her shoulders as she did it.

"You're an artist, Meg. I am a real estate developer. What job could we possibly have to discuss? You wanna make weirdo abstract sculptures to put out in front of my condos?"

She punched my shoulder. "I paint, you jackass. And no. I want you to hire me as your secretary."

My jaw dropped. "What?"

"You need a secretary, and I need a job."

I shook my head to try to clear it. "Wait. First, why do you need a job? You just a did a show, and Candace said it was a major success."

Candace and Jack had, in fact, dragged me to the show. And I'd bought a painting of hers. Meg thought I'd bought it for the office, but actually, it hung in a prominent spot in my bedroom. I would never tell her, but I really liked the damn thing.

"It doesn't matter why," she said forcefully. "I just need a job, a good paying job."

"But you are not a secretary," I pointed out.

"I used to be."

"What?"

"Yeah, all through college."

I had more excuses up my sleeve, and I was going to need to use every single one of them. "I need more than a secretary, Meg. I'm the CEO. I need an executive assistant. A few years of—"

"I worked as the assistant for Rick Hoffman for two years. You can call him if you need a reference."

My jaw dropped again. Rick Hoffman was a well-known investment banker in San Francisco. He was famous for only hiring the best people and being a real hard ass.

"Why would he hire a college kid?"

"Look, just call him for a reference. When you get it, and it's excellent—which it will be—can I have the job, or not?"

"Why don't you just go back to Rick?"

She rolled her eyes and put a hand on her hip. "Because he'll want a multi-year commitment. And I am only doing this for as long as it takes to get the money I need. And you're my best friend's brother-in-law so I'm asking for a favor here."

I was a little surprised she willingly admitted she was asking for a favor. And I was about to revel in the reality that she may, in fact, be halfway human.

But then she ruined it. "Besides, you clearly need me. You are a complete fucking disaster. I can start on Monday." Meg held out her hand as if for me to shake it.

I stared down at her tiny palm in the dim light. It waited, soft and elegant with intricately painted fingernails, to accept my own. "But you hate me."

"Don't remind me, rich boy. But I'm willing to overlook it. Do we have a deal or not?"

Perhaps it was the stench of the Dumpsters and my desire to be away from them, maybe it was the crisp night air affecting my thinking, or it could have been her beautiful form outlined in the evening light. But I shook her hand.

Chapter 2

Meg sat across from me in my office on Monday morning. As the new CEO of Morrison and Sons, I had the largest one. It was my dad's old office. Every once in a while, the massive room, with the oversized expensive furniture, made me feel fit for the job. But most of the time, it just intimidated me.

Meg, on the other hand, created a completely different set of feelings in me. She wore a sleeveless silk blouse, a wide, flouncy skirt that landed above her knees, and a pair of strappy sandals. Behind my mahogany desk, I hid an erection which had sprung up just from watching her walk into the room.

Her long black hair shifted over one shoulder as she leaned forward and picked up the nameplate on my desk. One painted fingernail tapped against the brass. "Hayden R. Morrison. What does the *R* stand for?"

I looked into those huge, round eyes and answered automatically. "Robert."

"Hmmm," she said, plopping the nameplate noisily on the desk before leaning back.

I looked down at the folder in front of me with her intake paperwork from HR. I had, in fact, called Rick Hoffman, and he'd given her a stellar reference. I'd also asked him why he'd hired a college student to be his executive assistant. He said that she'd started in the mailroom and worked her way up. A real go-getter he'd called her. He'd said it was tragic that art had taken her away from what could have been an incredible career in the corporate world.

"What does the *C* stand for?" I asked, turning the tables. "It says here your name is C. Megan Kahele."

She pursed her lips. "What does it matter?"

I flipped through the file. "Well, there must be a copy of your social security card in here so…"

"Fine. It's Charley."

"Charley? Your real first name is Charley?"

"Yes. I'm not really a fan. Hence, I go by Megan, or Meg."

"Huh."

"Yeah, interesting," she said flatly. "So, I assume that's my desk out there." She pointed behind her with her thumb toward the foyer-like entrance space in front of my office that held a large desk and a comfortable chair.

"Yes."

"And I suppose the job is basically to organize your life for you?"

"Um…yeah. I guess."

"Great." She stood. "I take one twenty-minute break in the morning, an hour lunch, and a twenty-minute break in the afternoon. I don't work after five without double pay, and I don't like tea, only coffee. So, if you like coffee, I will get you a cup when—and only when—I am getting some for myself." With those demands declared, she walked out of my office, shutting the door behind her.

And I sat there wondering, what the hell had I gotten myself into?

I knew I didn't deserve my job. The people who

worked for me knew it, too. And as a close friend of the family, I was sure Meg was well aware of my inadequacies, making it all the more bizarre that she'd offered to work for me.

My father spent his twenties working his ass off to help my grandfather build an empire. As a result, he didn't settle down with my mom and start having kids until his mid-thirties. So, he'd reached retirement age when I was only twenty-nine, meaning that I had to take over the entire company at a relatively young age. A task no one thought I was up to.

I'd turned thirty a week before Chelsea's rehearsal dinner, but I was still one of the youngest CEOs in the business. Regardless of my age, it was never supposed to be this way. Jack was not only the oldest son, he had also showed the most promise. Smart and savvy, Jack had gone to business school as soon as he'd graduated, with honors of course, from preparatory school. But then, halfway through college, Jack had flipped out. He'd left San Francisco for five years and came back a raging hippy. He'd used his trust fund to start a nonprofit that helped homeless people and poor tenants. He'd gone after us, his own family.

With Jack out of the picture, my dad turned to my baby sister, Chelsea, to take over the reins of the company. I didn't blame him. I left high school with sub-par grades and went on to get a degree in Liberal Arts at a party school. I was no one's hope for the future. After school, my dad gave me a fake job, Vice President of Internal Organizational Operations—whatever the hell that meant.

In that job, I picked my own assignments. And wouldn't you know it, the very first assignment, I came right up against my brother, and he beat the pants off me. So clearly, we were all just waiting for Chelsea to take over.

Then, a few years ago, Chelsea announced that she was giving up her birthright to the company to be a filmmaker. She was good at it, too. She made killer documentaries, and I was proud as shit of her.

But with a bachelor uncle, aging himself, that left the kingdom to me. So, I'd gotten my MBA, put my playboy ways behind me, and stepped up. I was scared shitless on the day my dad had handed over the helm to me. And six months later, I was still shaking in my boots.

Fortunately, I had a great set of executives and support staff around to save my ass all the time. And, much to my surprise, Meg fit right in. She excelled at her job. She always made sure I was briefed before every meeting and I had exactly the right materials in my hand when I walked into it. She never let me miss a beat. She was a true professional, a secretary worthy of a much better CEO.

On her third day at work, she got a real taste of what it was like to work for me. Late in the afternoon, Jacob Wheeler stormed into my office. He threw the door open, slamming it against the doorstop on the wall. His large frame waltzed through the opening, his ample belly leading. His light blue eyes were on fire, and he wore a deep frown on his hard face.

"What the fuck, Hayden?" he bellowed.

Meg raced in, right on his heels. "Excuse me, *sir*," she said sternly. "Do you have an appointment?"

He looked at her for a brief moment, as if she were a complete lunatic. Then he turned back to me. "What is this?" He hooked his thumb over his shoulder.

The guy was a real asshole. "*She* is my new executive assistant, Jacob. Please treat her with respect." I used my most commanding voice.

He smirked.

I turned my attention away from him. "Meg, this is the VP of Operations. He's been here since before I was born, and he thinks he owns the place. But he doesn't. *I do.*" I pierced Jacob with my gaze.

Jacob made no secret of the fact that he didn't approve of me being CEO. He ardently believed he should have been given the job. During the transition, he'd actually sat in this very office and told my father, with me sitting right beside him, that I would fuck it up.

My dad had told him if he had wanted to ascend to CEO, he should have worked for a publicly traded company, not a family-owned one. My father had never hidden his intention to turn the reins of Morrison and Sons over to one of his children. He'd also told Jacob he didn't have the people skills to do the job. That was a deeply truthful statement.

Jacob slammed a folder down on my desk and pointed his finger at my face. "I just got this bullshit from HR. You're giving Phoebe my job."

"You reach full retirement in two months, Jacob, and we agreed you would be leaving at that time. I think we both know the less time you and I work together, the better," I said, reminding him of the conversation we'd had that day in this very office when it had still belonged to my father.

"Sure, but, *Phoebe*? The chick who currently runs customer service? She's a little punk—" He stopped himself, and I knew he wanted to say, "—like you."

After five years at the company, Phoebe had proven she could handle the job. She was highly educated, motivated, hard-working, and competent. I was completely confident in my decision to promote her.

But I didn't feel the need to explain myself to Jacob. So I simply said, "Phoebe is very capable. And the decision is *mine*. Not yours."

"I'm not training her," he said, sounding like the childish bully he was.

"You don't have to. She's in executive training now, and after that she'll work with Greg and Hillary to get caught up on the mechanics of the job."

I'd had no intention of exposing my new VP of Operations to Jacob's vitriol. So I had made plans to work around him. I saw that register on his face. I was making him a lame duck for the remainder of his time here. He didn't like it.

He turned red. His eyes narrowed. I could see the tantrum forming. Out of the corner of my eye, I saw Meg move to the side of the room, where she could see both him and me better. She watched the entire exchange with hawk-like eyes.

Jacob leaned over my desk, planting his palms in front of me. "You know what, Hayden?" he sneered. "You and your little *girls*"—he threw his head to the side, toward Meg—"are going to run this place into the ground. And I'm going to laugh my ass off when that happens. And your dad will have gotten exactly what he deserves."

I stood. In that moment, I was no longer trying vainly to defend myself against this man and his partly accurate attacks on me. Now I faced a bully who intended to drag Meg and Phoebe down with me. And one of those smart, capable women stood right there in the room, watching all of it go down.

It brought out a whole new side of me. "Here's the deal, Jacob," I said calmly.

He straightened up, and we faced one another, my desk standing between us, our forms, nearly the same in mass but built very differently, were mimicking one another, arms at our sides, hands balled into fists, shoulders tight, backs straight.

"You have two months till you get your full retirement benefits. You can either keep your mouth shut for the next eighty days and do that, or take the offer I made to you when I took over."

I'd offered him an early-out package, a generous one. But he wanted to take another job after this. He wanted to get that elusive CEO position somewhere. And if he took the early-out, it would be a sign that he couldn't cut the transition. People would know I wanted him gone.

"Or," I said, my voice turning dark, "I can just fire your ass right here, right now. What's it gonna be?"

He stared at me for a beat. Then he grunted. His whole body moving with it. "Well, I'll be damned," he said slowly. "You grew a pair."

"Get out of my office, Jacob."

"All right. I'll be nice." His smirk was surprisingly absent as he acquiesced.

He turned and walked toward the door of my office. He paused to look over at Meg. From my angle, I couldn't see the face he made as he glared at her. But she didn't need my help. She pulled her hand up and gave him the finger. He grunted again and walked out the door.

I was still standing in exactly the same place. Meg moved first. She shifted on her feet and headed toward the door. She paused and turned to me. "Badass, Hayden. Very badass," she said, before walking out and shutting the door behind her.

****

Two months and three weeks ago

Meg was the best secretary I'd ever had. In just one week's time, she'd proven she was completely up to the challenge of organizing my life. She even made sure I had a wedding gift in my hand and was in my tux, in a limo, on my way to pick up my date twenty minutes early on the day of Chelsea's wedding.

If only I'd let her pick my date, too. I looked over at Shanda. We sat at a table right in front of the long head table, Shanda on one side of me and Jack across from me. My niece lay, sound asleep, in Jack's arms and on his other side his wife, Candace, leaned toward me, her eyes bright.

The difference between Candace and Shanda was night and day. Candace was graceful and charming. A successful lawyer at Morrison and Sons, Candace had built an incredible career while balancing a husband—who was not, in my opinion, entirely stable—and a new baby. She was also stunningly beautiful. I'd spent a good three years of the last seven pining for her. Shortly after her second wedding anniversary with my brother, I'd gotten my shit together and put away my feelings for Candace.

But that didn't stop me from comparing her to other women. I couldn't help it. My brother had scored the ultimate woman as his lifelong companion and the mother of his child. I wanted one, too.

Shanda was a looker, I supposed. Though instead of a sexiness born from dignity and high-class beauty, she had giant boobs spilling out of a very, very low-cut dress. Also, she had a great ass, and absolutely everyone could see it in her tight, very, very short dress. Her hair was large, hard, and weirdly shiny. And she was loud as hell. Her voice carried across the room as she told an off-color story involving G-strings and gelatin to Henry's cousin Danny in a high-pitched voice that made it sound like she was being tortured. I tried to tune her out as I focused on Candace's story.

"I was supposed to pick Grace up at the airport yesterday. Sandy and I were in the pick-up lot waiting for her to call me and say she had her bags and was ready to be picked up at the curb, right? But when she called, she said she was boarding another plane and I should go home," Candace said.

"Where was she going?" I asked.

"She didn't say at the time. She said she was getting on a plane, she was fine, and I shouldn't worry. She called me like fourteen hours later from Rio."

"Rio? Wait. I'm confused." I leaned forward, my arms resting on the table, sheer curiosity pulling me toward Candace and the story she was telling.

"We were, too," Jack told me.

"I thought she was living in Sweden with her husband and was flying in to SF for a couple of weeks. She planned to come to the wedding, right?" This was as much I knew about Candace's other best friend.

Candace nodded. "Yeah, but something's been up for the last couple of months. Every time I talked to her, she was cavorting around some other European country alone. I kept telling her to come home, or that I'd meet her somewhere, but she said no."

"So." Jack leaned toward me, conspiracy shining in his eyes. "Now she's in Rio." He paused for dramatic effect, and his eyebrows rose. "With Meno."

"Meno? The guy you stayed with when you dropped out of college?" I asked Jack.

"That's the one," he confirmed.

"So…is there something going on between them?"

Candace and Jack exchanged a look. But before either of one of them could answer my query, a pair of thin, pale arms snaked around my neck.

"Hayden, I want to dance," Shanda whined.

I patted her forearm. "It's not time yet, sweetheart. We have to wait until Henry and Chelsea have had the first dance."

"Awwww. But I want to dance now."

"I tell you what." I extracted myself from her and stood. "I'll dance with you when I get back from the restroom."

This seemed to appease her, and she sat back down. I made my escape.

I left the ballroom and headed down the same narrow hallway I'd used a week before. Once again, I ran into Meg. This time she leaned up against the wall, her head thrown back, her cell phone in pieces on the floor in front of her.

Chapter 3

"Aaaarrrgggghhhh!" she screamed, pounding her fists into the wall behind her.

I approached her slowly, like a wild animal. "Meg, are you okay?"

Her head snapped up and her eyes narrowed. She looked downright scary as she glared at me. "No."

"Um." I stepped forward again, hesitantly. "Can I help?"

"Nice date," she said dryly. "Where the hell did you find her?"

I scratched my chin. "Um, actually, at a strip club."

She laughed. "Really?"

I grinned. "Yep. Can't you tell?"

She nodded her head in an exaggerated move. "Oh yeah. That was my first guess."

"So, um…what did your cell phone do to deserve this?" I looked down at the battered device, which lay in several pieces at her feet.

She glanced at it briefly before looking back up at me. "You are the rich, good-looking CEO of a major corporation. Why the hell would you need to bring a stripper to your sister's wedding?"

I took another step so I stood across from her and leaned against the opposite wall. "I have relationship problems."

Her brow raised. "Really? What kind of

problems?"

I didn't really want to get into this, especially with my secretary. But she was obviously not interested in talking about whatever was going on with her, and I didn't see any way to extract myself from this conversation without risking some sort of violent retribution.

I shrugged. "My parents really want me to get married. Jack's married. As of today, my baby sister is married. And here I am, the new CEO—who could seriously use some credibility, I might add—and I have no marriage prospects. So, they're on me all the time. Truth is, I'm no good at picking out a future wife."

"So…the stripper is because…"

I ran my hand through my hair. It was getting long around the ears. I either needed a haircut, or I had to commit to growing it out. The trouble was, I couldn't make a decision lately to save my life, not even about my stupid hair.

"It was easier than finding someone else. I knew if I asked she would come, and she won't expect me to call her tomorrow for another date." My shrug reflected how pathetic I was.

She stared me for a long time, examining me. Then her face lit up. "I've got an idea!"

"Whoa. You just did a one-eighty. What's happening?" I tried to keep up.

She reached down and picked up the pieces of her phone. She shoved them into her small handbag and straightened up. "I'll tell you over drinks. Come on."

I followed Meg back into the dining room and over to the bar. "Wait, I never went to the men's room," I told her as she pushed me toward the open bar.

"You didn't have to go. You were just trying to get away from shake-it-Shanda over there."

She was right, of course, so I didn't argue as she ordered two Scotch and sodas and shoved one into my hand.

"How do you know I like this?" I asked.

"There's a bottle of Scotch in your bottom desk drawer," she replied.

Before I could accuse her of rifling through my desk, she pulled me through the french doors that exited one end of the dance floor onto the patio. A string of lights illuminated the wooden decking but left enough darkness for the shadows of the hills in the distance and the shimmer of moonlight reflected on the bay.

"My idea." Meg called my attention back to her.

"Right. Let's hear it."

"Hire me."

"I already hired you."

"No, I mean, hire me to be your matchmaker." She sounded exasperated because I hadn't read her mind.

"Instead of my secretary?"

"No. *In addition* to being your secretary."

"How much money do you need?" I was starting to really wonder about her financial situation.

"Never mind about that, rich boy." She waved her hand dismissively. "Here's the deal. I will find you a wife. On the day you propose marriage to her, you owe me a finder's fee of $15,000."

I'm sure she expected me to balk at the amount. The fear was clear in her eyes as she said the number, and her voice quivered just a little. I might not be a great businessman, but I could read people, even someone like Meg with a million brick walls erected around herself.

I gave her credit for throwing the number out there with confidence, despite her nervousness. And $15,000 wasn't a lot, not to me. So I brushed past that and went on to negotiations.

"Even if she says no?" I asked.

She rolled her eyes. "Fine, only if she says yes. In the meantime, I'll charge a retainer…let's say…equivalent to my current salary."

"Wait. You're just trying to get me to pay you double."

"For double the work," she pointed out, looking innocent as shit in the moonlight. "I'll be your loyal secretary, *and* I'll find you a wife."

I leaned back against the railing and regarded her. I took a sip of my drink and chewed it over. The money didn't mean anything to me. Between my salary and my trust fund, not to mention my share of the company profits, I had more of it than I knew what to do with. Meg was obviously desperate for cash. I wanted to ask her why she didn't just ask Candace for a loan or me for that matter. But I think I understood that to this woman, pride was a physical being.

I could help Meg. And while I doubted she would actually be able to find my future wife, it couldn't hurt to let her try.

"How long do you expect this to take?" I asked casually, as if we were making an ordinary business deal, rather than talking about my life.

She chewed on her bottom lip. "I'm not sure. But fast. Because you need a wife, and I need the money."

I stepped forward, putting myself within inches of her. She smelled like flowers and soft light. I held out my hand. "Deal."

Meg shook my hand, and then, without another word, she turned on her heel and walked back into the reception hall. I leaned against the railing, staring out at the darkened bay, breathing in the crisp night air.

I wasn't alone for long. The glass door opened, and I turned to find Henry.

"Hey, brother," he said, slapping me on the back.

I grinned at him. "Hi, Henry." I shook his hand. "I really am glad you married my baby sister. I mean that."

Henry was a perfect match for Chelsea. Smart and funny, Chelsea could accomplish anything in life, but until recently, she'd lacked the self-confidence for some of it. A rock star's son with the looks of a model, Henry was sweet and down-to-earth. Most important, he was completely smitten with Chelsea. His affection had finally proven to her she was just as amazing as we'd always told her she was.

"Thanks. I'm pretty freaking happy about it, too," he said.

"You two are perfect for each other." It showed in the way they looked at each other, both with that indescribable expression that was at once longing and possession.

"Is…uh…is everything all right?" he asked me.

"Huh." I grunted. "I think I just got myself into something."

"With Meg or your date?"

"Meg." Her name left my lips on a sigh.

"Really?" His brows raised in surprise.

"Not like that," I said quickly.

I examined him. Framed by the glass door at his

back, he stood tall and handsome in his tux. His face held the look of a man completely happy with his life. I wanted to have that look on my face.

I sighed again. "You know I hired Meg to be my secretary, right?"

Henry nodded.

"Well, I think I just hired her to be my matchmaker, too."

He laughed. "You *think*."

"She's kind of a force to be reckoned with," I told him. And that's exactly what I was thinking. Meg had bowled me over, again.

"True," he agreed.

"She talked me into letting her find me a potential wife. For a fee, of course."

This made him look even more surprised. "What?"

I didn't know why, but I needed a confidant. My relationship with my own brother was too complicated. So in my weak moment, I turned to my brand new brother-in-law to be my shoulder to lean on.

"I need to settle down," I told him. "I'm the CEO of the company now. I need stability. I can't be running around with girls like Shanda." I gestured to the dining room that could be seen through the window behind him. He turned slightly, just in time to see my date riding on his cousin's lap.

He turned back to me. "No argument there. She might end up in a fight with Danny's boyfriend, you know."

I laughed, and the sound was filled with a lightness I didn't feel. My life was a freaking mess.

"Do you think Meg can do it? Find you a great little woman?" he asked.

I shrugged. "Probably not. But it could be entertaining to let her try. Besides, she obviously needs the money."

We were both silent for a long moment. Perhaps he was thinking about Meg's money troubles. Or perhaps he was still back in that dining room with his wife. The thought made me look past him through the glass door.

"Should be interesting," Henry said thoughtfully.

I saw my sister, looking gorgeous in her long white dress, step into the center of the dance floor alone. "I think you gotta go, man."

Henry whirled around and hustled through the door. I followed him, but split off as he headed to join Chelsea. I moved to the outskirts of the dance floor instead, blending into the audience.

Henry's dad started to sing. Chelsea's husband scooped her up and they floated gracefully across the floor. I smiled because my baby sister looked so happy. I loved her, and I was glad she had found a partner, a companion, someone to help her make all her dreams come true.

But inside I was breaking. I needed a partner, too. I needed someone to support me as I took on a job way too big for me. Someone to kill the loneliness I'd felt most of my adult life. But for some reason, I didn't think it was in the cards for me.

****

Two months and two weeks ago

I was so thankful Meg had come along. I wasn't sure she'd believe what a train wreck this whole thing had turned out to be if she hadn't seen it for herself. Because she'd come along, she stood as witness to the fact that this ride through Dante's seventh level of hell on an out-of-control mine cart was not my fault.

The woman didn't move a muscle as I pulled her from her position draped over my shoulder and placed her gently onto the bed of the hotel room before turning to look at Meg. "Anything else?"

"Fuck," Meg said for the thousandth time. "I guess we should maybe leave her a note."

"Is it safe to leave her alone?" I asked, looking back at the blonde lying motionless on the bed. She was covered in her dinner and sleeping peacefully.

Meg walked over to her and took a closer look. "She took her own prescription. I called the pharmacist listed on the bottle. They said she would be okay."

I ran a hand through my hair. I'd been completely panicked when Tina started to act like she was under-the-table drunk, even though she'd been drinking nothing but diet soda all night. But then Meg informed me she'd taken an anti-anxiety pill just before I'd arrived.

"Yeah, but…how much did she take?" I asked, still feeling extremely worried about the whole thing.

"She only took one pill. But as soon as she'd thrown it into the back of her throat, she told me they make her super sleepy."

"Jesus. My date actually drugged herself." I groaned.

Meg laughed.

I glared at her. "Really? You think this is funny? This is *your* fault, you know." I waved at the woman she'd set me up with.

"I know, I'm sorry," she said between bouts of laughter. "It's just so…" She swiped at the tears running down her cheeks.

I rolled my eyes. "Let's leave this note already, and go get a drink," I grumbled, looking around the room for one of those hotel notepads and pen.

"Here, I got it," Meg said, finally regaining her freaking senses and leaning over the bedside table.

She scribbled for a while before I asked, "What are you writing?"

She read the note aloud to me. "*You passed out. We parked your car in the hotel garage, and we got you this room. Call me in the morning if you need help getting home.*" Meg stood and looked at me. "And I left your name and number."

"Are you kidding me? After tonight, you're going to make me drive her back to freaking Vallejo?"

She laughed and walked toward me. "Relax, Hayden. I left *my* name and number." She bit her lip and looked back at Tina. "On second thought, maybe I should stay in the other bed. That way I can keep an eye on her and be here in the morning to explain." She glanced at the second queen that sat empty to our right.

"That does seem safer. But—" I said, raising a finger, "—the drink part…"

She grabbed my elbow. "Is still on. Let's go."

Chapter 4

I had to admit, with a beer in my hand and the view of a smiling Meg across from me, my disastrous night seemed much more amusing.

"And then she said, 'Whoops! That usually makes me pass out.' " Meg's eyes were wide as she recalled her conversation with Tina in the restaurant bar.

"My favorite part was when, right in the middle of dinner, she just fell asleep on her plate of spaghetti. I thought I must be the most boring date ever at that point."

Meg laughed. "That was amazing timing. It was right when you were talking about your job."

I shook my head. "What the hell were you thinking setting me up with her?"

She shrugged. "I met her at a gallery opening last month. She's pretty, well-put-together, and seemed nice." She pulled a clump of her dark hair over her shoulder to play with it. My fingers twitched. I wondered how soft and silky it would feel sliding between my thumb and forefinger. "She's a lawyer. I don't know. She seemed perfect."

"Except that just the thought of going out with me causes her great anxiety."

"You *are* intimidating," she said, a smirk on her face.

"Baby, I am many things. Intimidating is not one of

them," I purred in my low, sexy voice.

Meg was unaffected. "I disagree, rich boy." She shook her head. "You're smart, successful, *rich*. Some girls are very intimidated by that. Plus, anyone who's ever heard of you knows you are a terrible man whore. That right there can be very intimidating to some women."

"I am *not* a man whore," I protested.

"Really? How many–"

"I am not discussing this." I shut down that conversation before it could get started. Then I turned the tables on her. "I hope that wasn't your best shot."

Meg took a leisurely pull from the two black skinny straws floating in her margarita glass before leaning back in her chair and smiling at me. "Don't worry, Bobby. I've got many more tricks up my sleeve. This was just a warm up."

"Some warm up." I took a sip of my beer, deciding if I wanted to ask. Then I decided I did. I set the beer down on the table between us with an audible clap. "Bobby?"

She grinned. Her huge brown eyes crinkled at the corners. I was beginning to figure out that was a sign of mischief. "Yeah, Hayden Robert Morrison is too damn formal. It reminds me of the playboy rich kid I hate."

"I *am* the playboy rich kid you hate," I pointed out.

"Exactly. And here I am having to work with you—"

"Technically you work *for* me. And you don't *have* to. It was your idea." I pointed my finger at her, accusing.

"Whatever. The point is, I need to think of you differently to preserve my dignity. See, I can hang out with a dude named Bobby."

She was ridiculous sometimes. But instead of turning me off, it intrigued me. I leaned forward, planting my elbows on the table. "What's your problem with rich people, anyway?"

She rolled her eyes and picked up her drink. A couple weeks ago, her attitude would have caused me to give up on the line of questioning. But I was not intimidated by her anymore. I was not afraid to push her buttons. She could call me all the names she wanted. It only egged me on.

"No, seriously. Candace told me you had some major problem with people with money. But she didn't elaborate," I pressed.

"Maybe it's just because I don't have any money myself."

"Not buying it," I told her.

She finished her drink in one long gulp and stood, slamming the glass on the table. "I need to check on your date. Thanks for paying for our hotel room," she said icily. "Goodnight, Hayden." She spun around on her heel and stalked away.

I didn't argue. I didn't follow her, either. I just watched that beautiful ass as she walked away from me and wondered if, despite her last words, she was actually starting to not hate me.

****

Two months ago

Meg, Kelly, and I stood in one corner of the popular bar at a stand-up table trying to talk over the din of after-work compatriots enjoying a drink.

I looked over at my date. I kind of understood why Meg had chosen her. She was beautiful, in the populist sense. Apparently, she'd done some modeling. That wasn't hard to believe. At almost six feet with her heels on, she was just a couple inches shorter than me, but towered over Meg, who stood a foot below me at my side. Kelly's hourglass shape and thin appendages were complemented by her wavy dyed-blonde hair.

Part of the reason Meg had chosen her was because she worked in real estate. Apparently, Kelly was the leasing agent for Meg's apartment building. Which, on the scale of the real estate world put her at the dollar store, whereas I ran a high-end department store by comparison.

I didn't care about that. In fact, I wasn't really interested in dating someone in the same line of work as me anyway. But I had figured it wouldn't hurt to go along with the date to keep Meg happy.

However, things were taking a wrong turn.

"As a real estate professional—" Kelly said airily.

I suppressed an eye roll.

"—I have to ask about the recent turnabout at Morrison and Sons. It's all anyone is talking about!"

It wasn't recent. It was about seven years in the making. But people in the business were still whispering about it in their break rooms as if it were a Hollywood affair.

I was used to questions about this. "Sure. Go ahead and ask." I took a long sip of my drink.

"Your father and grandfather built an empire. They bought up whole neighborhoods in San Francisco when they were still affordable. Then they waited until the right moment, tore down the old buildings, and built condo high-rises. They made a killing. They were kings of real estate. Legends!" She grew excited talking about my family history.

I nodded. "Yes," I agreed calmly.

"Then, after your brother lost his mind, everything changed."

I could talk about my brother's crazy-ass behavior, but it was another thing altogether to have someone else do it. I leaned forward. "You don't know my brother," I said quietly.

"Okay." She half apologized. "I don't. But setting that aside. You changed the whole company. You and your father did a one-eighty."

"That's right. Now we renovate historic buildings, and instead of selling them, we manage them ourselves. We make the profits from rentals, and we control the upkeep of the buildings. We've changed the way the company makes a profit, but we still make one."

She looked exasperated. "Okay. Let's talk about that building in the Mission District you just finished."

I smiled. I was particularly proud of that project. My dad and I had worked on that together before he retired, and we'd done a hell of a job, if I did say so myself. "Yes?"

"It was built in the seventies or something, right?"

"The late sixties," Meg said, surprising me. In her short time at the company, she'd learned a lot about it. It made me unexpectedly happy.

"Okay. The point is, it's ugly as sin. Instead of tearing it down, you renovated it. The thing was only like one-third full of tenants. You could have gotten rid of them, razed the building, and started over."

"We could have," I said calmly. "But we didn't. Instead we temporarily relocated the tenants while we restored it to its historic condition. Then we put the original tenants back in at the same rental rates and filled the building up. It has a long waiting list now. People are begging for a spot. And the new tenants are willing to pay market price for it. So I guess not everyone thinks it's an eyesore."

Her manner abruptly changed from being overly critical of my company to being overtly seductive. She leaned over the table and placed her hand over mine. "God. Your business brain is so sexy." Her gaze raked me up and down in a way that only women who were used to getting what they wanted did. "It matches the rest of you."

I turned to look at Meg. Her wide eyes made her look like a deer caught in headlights. I couldn't stop the smile that spread across my face. I turned back to Kelly because she was still talking.

"In fact, Hayden, I think you and I could really have a future. I know that's what you're looking for. Meg told me what this is all about, finding you a wife. I'd like to put my hat in the ring. We could make a hell of a team."

The truth was, this woman saw me as her meal ticket. She didn't just want to marry me; she wanted to be a part of my company. And no doubt she thought insulting the way my family and I operated showed her business prowess. This was a job interview with a side of sex. I couldn't get away fast enough. After pulling my hand out from under hers, I moved back from the table and pulled my wallet out of my back pocket.

Meg took over the talking at that point. She did what she did at work all the time, she read my mind and then fulfilled my needs exactly.

"Well, Kelly, thank you so much for meeting us

here," Meg said as I pulled a crisp fifty-dollar bill out of my wallet and set it under the salt shaker on the table to cover the bill and the tip. "I'm sure Hayden appreciated the opportunity to get to know you a little."

After quickly sending a text to Jack, I placed my hand on the small of Meg's back and moved us both away from the table. "I'll call you," Meg said over her shoulder.

Kelly tried to say something. But I moved faster toward the door, ignoring whatever it was.

"I'm so sorry," Meg said as we burst outside.

"It's not your fault."

My hand was still on her back, and I liked it there so I used my other hand to check my phone. I read Jack's return text as I gently steered her to a crosswalk.

She swiveled her head. "This is Sansome. We're going the wrong direction."

The light changed, and I moved us both across the street. We'd walked to the bar from the office right after work, and I supposed Meg expected me to take her back there. But I had other plans.

"Jack's office is not far from here. He hasn't left yet, and I wanted to stop by. Would you mind coming there with me?"

"Sure," she said easily. "But can I ask why?"

I looked ahead at the sidewalk as I answered her. "When someone digs on Jack or the company and what we're up to these days, I like to talk to Jack. He has a way of putting things into perspective." The solid truth just came flowing out of me. It was like that with Meg, and I didn't know why.

"Sounds perfect. I'm so sorry she was such an asshole. I couldn't believe she was ripping on the company. And calling your brother crazy. What the hell? *I* can call him crazy, and *you* can call him crazy. But *she* doesn't get to!"

I chuckled because I'd thought exactly the same thing. But I didn't want Meg to be too hard on herself. "You didn't know she'd do that. Besides, she seemed like a good pick. Same line of work. All that."

"And gorgeous," she pointed out.

I shrugged. "I guess."

"Seriously! She's a freaking model. She is objectively beautiful."

"Beauty is in the eye of the beholder," I said, looking down at her.

"So, tell me. What's beauty to you?"

"I like all kinds of women," I said, avoiding her question.

"Sure. But give me the description of your ideal hottie."

I hesitated and pulled her along as I made another turn toward Jack's building.

"Come on, Bobby," she coaxed.

I sighed, but complied. "Okay. I guess I tend to be attracted to shorter women, curvy women. Women who hold themselves with grace and confidence but don't necessarily know how deeply attractive they are." I looked straight ahead as I described Meg perfectly.

"Okay, good to know." Her voice sounded off, but I didn't look at her to see what facial expression went along with it.

"I feel like you're making me spill my guts today. Why don't you tell me what you are attracted to?"

We were on Jack's street now, so I slowed down while Meg chewed on her lip and contemplated my request.

"I've been with a variety of guys," she finally said.

"That's the same cop-out answer I just tried to give you," I pointed out.

"Fine. I guess the ultimate fantasy man is tall, built, and completely self-absorbed." She laughed.

"Maybe you should give up the self-absorbed part," I teased.

"I'm trying, believe me."

"Anybody right now?"

"No. Like I said, I'm trying to give them up. Not just the self-absorbed ones, but men in general. For a while at least."

"Hmmm," I said thoughtfully. "Taking a break?"

"Yes. Precisely. My focus right now is on finding you the perfect woman."

We reached Jack's building, and I opened the door for her. She paused in the doorway and turned her head up to look at me. "You know, Bobby, this whole talking to your brother after defending his honor to some asshole woman you had a date with…"

"Yes?"

"It's hot," she said. Then she walked through the door.

Chapter 5

"Look, you got this," Meg said confidently. "Everything you need is in here." She slapped the folder on my desk. "And here." She tapped my forehead with two fingers.

"I really appreciate your help with this," I told her.

She shrugged. "It's my job."

"You've gone above and beyond."

"Maybe you've just had shitty secretaries in the past," she said casually. "You have low standards."

I ran a hand through my hair. "The truth is, I'm not always sure I'm up to this job. And having you around, helping me—"

"Hold up there, Bobby." She put her splayed hand in front of me. "You are absolutely up to this job. All of it. This project is a major bitch, that's all. It has a million moving parts, you've got six executives working on it, half of them hate each other and the other half are only partly competent. You are doing as well on this as your dad would have."

I wished I could believe that. "You don't know my dad."

Meg slammed her hand on my desk. "Bullshit!"

I jumped, startled.

"You know what? You are just internalizing all the crap other people said about you all your life. Or you're internalizing all the shit you *thought* other people were saying about you. You can't do that. Fuck other people. Fuck what they think."

I was shocked still. Perhaps it was ridiculous, but no one had ever said that to me, at least not like that. No one had ever suggested I could be as good as my dad. Everyone, from the company executives to my own mother, looked at me with pity and understanding, as if I was a little kid trying to ride a bike without training wheels for the first time.

But not Meg. The hard glint in her eye reflected the truth of her convictions. It was fierce. *She* was fierce. And I started to understand that hiring her was the best thing I'd ever done.

"Okay, then." She stood and headed toward the door. She stopped, her hand on the knob and turned back to me. "You'll do great today. And also, I have a new date for you."

"Oh?"

"Three times a charm. You'll love her. Is Friday okay?"

I nodded. She smiled and walked out of my office, closing the door behind her.

I sat there for a long minute looking at the brass door handle. Then I glanced at the clock. I had twenty minutes before the meeting. No amount of rereading the materials would prepare me for it.

I picked up the phone and dialed the number by heart. It rang four times, which meant he hadn't been sitting in his office when I called. Most likely, he'd been somewhere else in the large house. But when his office phone rang, it alerted him on his cell and he could go to his sanctuary to pick up the landline. It was a strange collaboration of new technology and old school tradition.

"John Morrison Senior." My father's deep voice echoed back to me the same words he'd used to answer that phone for decades.

I had always thought it was funny that he added that "Senior," especially since Jack, whose real name was John Morrison Junior, didn't use the name.

I supposed that I'd always been a little jealous of that. In my mind, my dad used the Senior as a sign of his pride in Jack. With Chelsea, he would put his hand on her upper back and smile, and we would all know he was proud of her. But I had no little quirk, no reassuring touch, no phrase that indicated that my father had pride and confidence in me.

"Hi, Dad."

"Hayden." I could never be sure. But when he said my name like that, with a lift at the end, I thought maybe he was happy to hear from me. "How are you, son?"

"Good, Dad. Good."

"You've got a big afternoon, yeah?"

I pictured my dad just then. He did not plan to come into the office today, so he was probably wearing jeans and a sweatshirt with one of two college logos on it, either his, Chelsea, and Jack's alma mater, or mine. He had most likely been sitting on the porch with my mother when I called. They'd taken to playing cards with the couple next door in the afternoons. Now he would be in his massive home office, leaned back in his leather chair.

"Yes. I'm going to take this company to the next level today, Dad," I said with a confidence I didn't feel.

"It's a solid project, Hayden. And it was all your

idea."

The stark truth was there in his voice, undeniable. He *was* proud of me.

"It could backfire, though," I hedged.

A long pause allowed my dad to take in my vulnerability and swirl it around for a moment. I could hear it in the breaths he took. "This is business. Things can always go wrong."

"There's a lot of money sunk into this project already," I said, voicing my fears.

"But you have a back-up plan." It's half question, half statement.

"I do." In fact, I'd stayed late the night before going over the plan with Meg. She'd sat across from me and listened to me as I presented my plans to her. We called it bouncing ideas. But really, I was using her as my test audience, my security blanket.

"Of course you do. And you won't need it anyway. You've got this, Hayden."

I sat up a little straighter. Maybe, between Meg and Dad, I could actually gather up the confidence to pull this off.

Two hours later, I'd made the biggest deal of my life. All of my execs had shaken my hand and offered congratulations. My father had called my cell to tell me how proud he was of me. My uncle had even sent me a text message. Everyone was on cloud nine.

Everyone but me.

Making the deal and actually being able to pull off the project were two completely different things. Practically shaking by the time I got to the sanctuary of my office, I stumbled by Meg's empty desk, deeply disappointed she wasn't sitting there. So I flew by and went into my office, closing the door tightly behind me. I ran a hand through my hair. It came back wet. Shit. I was sweating like a pig. How many people had noticed that?

Candace had been right by my side when I'd pitched the idea of an unprecedented historic renovation project to a set of potential investors. She had told me afterward that it was a thing of beauty to watch. She said I was amazing.

I was glad I'd managed to look smooth on the outside, because on the inside, I was a freaking wreck. I needed Meg. Where the hell was she?

I dropped the materials in my arms onto my desk and rounded it, plopping down in my chair. Meg had been right there, taking notes and pulling up the various charts on the projection screen. But afterward, when the investors had left and my staff had all gathered around celebrating, she'd disappeared.

I banged my finger on the track pad of my laptop, punishing it for my pain. I intended to send a message to Meg. I would tell her I needed her, and she'd better get her ass back here right away.

But I didn't make it that far, because she'd already sent me a message.

Shut down your computer. Go into the exec bathroom. Put on the clothes. Take the back stairs to the parking garage. Do it now!

I chose to follow those directions exactly and without question. Meg had not let me down once. She'd been my savior. So I did what she wanted. In the bathroom, I found a pair of my favorite worn jeans, my running shoes, and a brand-new Giants T-shirt.

I threw it all on, only mildly wondering how the

hell she'd gotten my clothes, then I ran down the back stairs.

When I got to my car, I saw her sitting there, looking like a dream in the passenger seat. With a goofy grin pasted on my face, I climbed in.

"Where to?"

She looked at me, that beautiful round face full of fire and mystery. "AT&T Park. Where else?"

I waited until we were about ten minutes into the drive before I asked my first question. "So…how did you know I love baseball? I don't remember mentioning it."

"Jack," she said simply.

"And the clothes?"

"Also Jack. I enlisted his help. But for the record, this was all my idea," she said proudly.

"Oh, I don't doubt that for a second."

"You deserve a night to let your hair down, especially after that meeting. So that's what we are going to do, Bobby. We're going to drink and watch baseball, and we are not going to talk shop once. Got it?"

I gave her a salute. "Yes, ma'am."

****

I was laughing so hard, tears were leaking out of the corners of both eyes.

"You think you could do better? I'd like to see you make a splash hit, moron!" Meg screamed at the poor, unsuspecting bastard who'd dared to taunt her favorite player.

She looked like an angry Hawaiian hula dancer. Except instead of wearing a grass skirt and a lei, she stood at my side in a V-neck Giants shirt framing her amazing figure and tapering down to a short cotton skirt that showed her bronzed legs. Above her big, beautiful eyes, her brows stood at sharp angles and her mouth formed a hard line. In case there was any doubt about her anger, her tiny fists were clenched and sat on her perfectly rounded hips.

I grabbed her hand and pulled her back into the seat beside me. There was a defiant squeak as she rammed herself roughly onto the folding chair.

"I think you taught him a lesson, Chuck." I wiped my eyes with the back of my hand.

"Chuck?"

"Yeah, it's short for Charley, your real name," I explained.

She laughed. "Wow. That's pretty good. Okay. You can call me Chuck. But only you." She pointed her finger at me.

"Here." I handed her the beer she'd shoved into my hands when she'd stood up to yell and scream.

She grabbed it and took a long gulp, then she looked at me. I was holding my own empty cup. "You need another."

I shook my head. "I've had quite a few, and it's the eighth inning. How the hell are we going to get home?"

Her eyes lit up. "I have an idea!"

"Oh God," I said, with pretend fear. In fact, I couldn't wait to hear her idea. And chances were, I would follow her no matter where she took us.

"Let's take the ferry to the East Bay!"

"What?" She must have been drunker than I'd thought.

She turned in her seat to face me more fully. "The ferry! It's so fun! It runs right after the game. It goes across the Bay in the dark. The bridge will be all lit up. Oh! And there's a bar right on the damn ferry! It's freaking fun!"

"So we land in Oakland?"

"Yeah. Or Alameda."

I chuckled. "So…since neither of us lives in the East Bay, what do we do then?"

"We go to the beach."

I shake my head. "What?"

"Alameda has a cool little beach."

"Are we going to sleep on this beach?"

"Nah. We could get a ride back."

"You're insane," I said, a giant grin on my face.

She ignored that. "Are you in?"

I looked at her. She was so full of fire. She lived her life as if it were one giant adventure. Despite that, no matter what crazy-ass thing we did until late into the night, she'd be at work in the morning, doing exactly what was expected of her.

Sitting there, watching my new, and unexpected, friend make plans for a night of ill-advised exploits, I wished I were more like Meg. In fact, I used to be. I had lived life by the seat of my pants once, chasing each thrill one day at time. But now I had responsibilities. I'd thought that meant I had to change who I was. But Meg's life stood as proof that wasn't necessarily the case.

Maybe Meg and I weren't the opposites we always thought we were. Maybe we had much more in common than either of us knew.

****

"I am pretty sure this beach is closed." I looked around at the completely empty area. Even lit only by the stars and the moon, I could see we were alone.

"It is. It's better this way. No one to bother us." Meg leaned back on her hands and looked out at the Bay.

I rubbed my heel in the sand, feeling its coarseness against my skin and copied her pose. We were side by side on a small hill, just out of reach of the surf.

"That was a fun ferry ride."

In the dark, I could see her grin. "I know all the ways to have a good time on a small budget."

"But you don't have to," I pointed out. "I could take you to any damn expensive thing you want."

The look on her face told me I'd made a mistake. She hated my money. It was best not to mention it. But more important, I'd made it sound it like I wanted to take her out, like a date, like a real date. And even though I wouldn't mind doing exactly that, Meg would.

I was still trying to find a way to recover from my mistake when she spoke. "Oh, you are going to spend money tonight, Bobby. There's no BART on this island, and the ferry is done running for the night. It's going to cost you a pretty penny for us to take a ride share back across the Bay." Her tone was mischievous, and I let out a sigh of relief.

"I don't know. I think my credit card is maxed out," I said.

She scoffed. "If that's actually possible, I'd like to know how you managed it."

I looked at her profile in the bluish-black night. Our relationship had been altered completely in the last few weeks. We'd become friends, but we'd also become strange confidantes. For some reason I still didn't fully understand, I felt like I could tell Meg anything. She, above all others, had seen me at my most unsure. She'd heard me confess my insecurities about my position at the company.

Stranger still, I couldn't bring myself to lie to her about anything. I didn't know if the feeling was mutual, or if my surety in that was because Meg seemed not to filter her thoughts, but instead to lay it all out on the line. This was a unique quality for me lately. Since I'd become the boss, everyone always told me what they thought I wanted to hear. But not Meg.

That's why I chose to ask her a very difficult question. "You think being rich fucked me up?"

She turned to look at me. "What?"

I shrugged. "I always wondered. But I never had anyone to ask until now."

"Why ask me?"

"Because you will be brutally honest."

She chuckled. "True. Also, you probably don't know anyone that grew up poor to ask."

"Candace," I pointed out.

Meg waved her hand dismissively. "She grew up middle class. *I* grew up poor as dirt."

I angled toward her. "Tell me about it."

"What's to tell? My mom was a single parent. She had me at fifteen. My dad was nowhere to be found. She got fixed right after so she wouldn't ever get pregnant again. She didn't like kids and never wanted any. When I was growing up, she worked nights. So I saw her for like two hours every day after I got home and before she went to work. She resented the shit out me because she had to work so hard to feed me. I took care of myself mostly and got a job as soon as it was legal. On my eighteenth birthday, when the paltry child-support checks quit coming from the dad I never met, she introduced me to the roommate she'd found for me and helped me pack my stuff."

"She kicked you out?"

"Pretty much. She couldn't wait to get rid of me so she could start her life over. She acts like a twenty-year-old now, drinking and partying all the time. I don't see her much."

I felt sad for her, hurt for her, and angry that she hadn't been loved and cherished like she should have been. "Fuck," I said softly.

"Now let's discuss this hang-up you have, Bobby. You grew up rich and you think it fucked you up?"

"I didn't say that. I just wondered if *you* thought that."

"I don't think you're fucked up," she said.

"Awwww. Thanks. That might be the nicest thing you've ever said to me."

"Shut up. No. Seriously. Your life is so amazingly on track. What, exactly, is fucked up about it?"

I had grown up not only rich but loved and cared for. I didn't feel like I could have this conversation with Meg anymore. She'd had a shit childhood. What did I have to whine about?

"Nothing. Forget I asked."

Meg sat up, crossed her legs, and turned fully toward me. "No, Bobby. I want to talk about this. I think you *are* fucked up."

"Wait, you just said I wasn't."

"I changed my mind."

I let out a bark of laughter. "Okay. Let's hear it," I challenged.

"You are fucked up because you have no idea how

great you are."

"Really?" I asked, intrigued now.

"Yeah. Take Jack. He may seem like the humble charity dude, right. He gave up his birthright and now he fights for justice. Blah, blah, blah. But he did all of that because he knew he *could* do it. He knew he was capable. *And* he knew, no matter what he did or how badly he screwed over his own family, you all would still love him."

I couldn't deny any of that was true.

"And Chelsea. Bless her heart. She's a giant dork. She looks like she probably hasn't had a self-confident thought in her life. But that's not true. Not at all. Chelsea is a freaking warrior who goes after exactly what she wants and gets it."

"True," I said softly, liking the way she'd described my little sister.

"You grew up in the same environment that produced both of them, but you are literally waiting for yourself to fuck up. You are, without a doubt, your biggest critic and most skeptical observer. *You*"—she pushed her index finger into my chest and leaned toward me—"don't see the potential everyone else sees in you. Now how the fuck did that happen?"

I stared at her in the shadows of the night. No one had ever seen me as clearly as she did. I shook my head slowly. "Middle child syndrome?" I asked, my voice rough and heavy.

"That's a cop-out. Here's what I think. I think maybe no one ever told you—or maybe they did and you weren't listening—that you are an amazing man, Hayden Morrison. You are smart and capable and driven and charming. You're even hot as hell. Which means that my job, to find you a wife, is going to be a piece of cake."

I had always found Meg attractive. But now she was so much more than that. She was sexy as hell. Combined with the warmth of her body and the soft shape of her lips in the glow of the moon, I was losing my mind.

I leaned forward. I was going to kiss Meg. For a moment, I thought she might let me. Her body seemed to drift closer to mine. We were on a collision course.

Then she jumped up. I pulled out of my reverie abruptly. I was still trying to catch up when she fished her phone out of her purse and ordered a ride.

"We gotta go, Bobby," she said tersely.

Chapter 6

Meg
Present day

I sit in the back of a limo, completely melting down. The driver must think I'm a lunatic. Though he never lets on.

I give him directions to a house I haven't been to in ages. I have completely fucked up my life, and I know what I need right now. I need to talk to a person who can help me sort out everything that's happened, someone who will listen without judging and without questioning my actions. In short, I need someone who is as much of a mess as I am.

The driver pulls in front of the house, and I let out a sigh of relief when I see the door swing open. I run into Grace's arms. She meets me on the doorstep and envelops me kindly. "Oh Meg," she says, softly.

Without saying anything further, she pulls me into the house and closes the door behind us. We pick our way through boxes, some already filled and taped up, others overflowing with clothes, all haphazardly waiting for some sort of organization. Eventually we reach the couch, which is still in its place against the far wall of the living room.

Grace sits me down and goes to the kitchen. She retrieves a bottle of wine and two glasses while I get my shit together. I manage to stop the racking sobs that have overtaken me for the last thirty minutes and wipe at my red and swollen eyes.

"Okay, sweetie. Here we go." She sits down beside me and places the wine and glasses on the coffee table. Then she pours us both a large glass and hands me one. With the other helping of the deep red liquid perched in her own grasp, she turns to me, her free hand gently rubbing my upper arm.

"Where is he?" I ask her, looking around the room.

"He went out to get more boxes. He'll be back in a little bit…Meg." She looks at me with wide eyes. Her beautiful blonde hair frames her perfect pale face. Concern is written all over it. "Tell me what's going on?"

"I…God, I'm sorry. You have your own problems to deal with." Suddenly, I feel terrible for burdening her with me. After all, she's in town to move out of her home, the home she shared with her husband, a husband that divorced her out of the blue.

"Don't be ridiculous. I'm fine. Better than fine." She smiles at me reassuringly. "But you, clearly, are not. So, tell me what's going on."

I stare into Grace's green eyes searching for comfort or wisdom or the answer to a question I haven't yet formed in my mind. She is not the person I would have expected myself to run to. She and I are friends, but only because we are both friends with Candace. She is our connection. Candace is my best friend. She's the one I would be expected to turn to.

But as much I love Candace, she isn't like me. She's practical and rational. She waited her whole life to find one man and fall madly in love with him. She got married and has a perfect life and a perfect little baby.

Grace is much more of a disaster, like me. She's childless and newly divorced. The day she found out her husband was leaving her, she boarded a plane to Brazil and shacked up with Jack's best friend, Meno.

Like me, Grace didn't have some master plan. She fell face first into the water of life. Only she didn't drown. She's happy. She's found a way to float.

Not me. I have been pulled under, and I can't see a way to the surface.

"I made a huge mistake," I tell her.

She nods. She understands. And that is why I am here. "A guy?" she asks, knowingly.

I nod. "You know me. I love assholes." I shrug. "But it was different this time. I didn't connect with another asshole. I didn't date some guy who was hot but who I didn't really care about, who didn't really care about me. This time it was the real thing. *He* was real. *We* were real. And I blew it."

She strokes my hair, from the top of my head, down to the tip that sits flush with the bottoms of my shoulder blades. "Tell me about it. Tell me what happened, Meg."

I take a deep breath. It rattles, like the bars of a cage. And I tell her.

****

One month and three weeks ago

There was something completely charming about Hayden's insecurity. When I watched him at work, I could see it plainly. We'd be in his office, going over something before a big meeting, and he would run his hand through his mousy brown hair. It was getting too long and when he did that the hair would flail in every direction. Then it would slowly settle down into smooth disarray.

His eyes would get this look, almost like panic. An intense blue color, they were wide and bright and looked like the sky was opening up to reveal all its secrets. His hands showed his anxiety, moving fast and frantic. Sometimes he would obsessively click his pen. Other times, he'd tap his fingers on the desk.

Then he would stand, push his chair out from his desk, and walk around it. And he would transform. Before leaving his office, where it was just me and him, he'd change into someone else, someone strong and confident, and not the least bit worried about how he was handling his family's legacy. When he walked out of that room, there was no hint that the world rested on his shoulders.

That's how he was on a date, too. Perfectly put together, his dress slacks and button-up shirt hugged his immaculately shaped body just right. Overly long or not, it looked like every hair sat exactly where it was supposed to be. It was late in the day, and he sported an amazing five o'clock shadow that was sexy as hell. His sharp eyes shone the color of sapphire. He moved his muscular body with purpose and poise.

It was no wonder women were intimidated by him.

"Tell me, Stephanie. Do you enjoy the insurance business?" he asked, his voice smooth, his tone pure interest.

"I…uh…I…yeah. I mean…it's a family business. So…" the poor thing stuttered.

I sighed. I was pretty convinced he had no idea he did this to women. "Stephanie is also a big tennis player," I interjected, trying to help.

Hayden sat across from his date. I sat to the side at the round table. He shifted his gaze to me, piercing me with it. I wanted to help, but it would be better if I stayed quiet. After all, I was here as a go-between. This was a simple drinks and appetizers after work kind of date. They were supposed to be getting to know each other. If it went well, I'd be able to stay in the background, unseen and unheard, and they would talk to each other.

It wasn't going well.

"Tennis. I see." Hayden moved his eyes away from me and back to her, but I saw the struggle there. He was not into her. This was not going to work.

"Yes. Do you play?" Stephanie asked nervously.

"No. In fact, I've never even seen a game played."

My jaw dropped. "What?"

Hayden turned to me, an amused expression on his face. "I haven't."

"What kind of rich dude doesn't play tennis, let alone watch it?"

I'd forgotten myself altogether. Stephanie was also from a fairly wealthy family. It's part of the reason I'd set them up. I figured they would have some things in common.

Teasing Hayden about growing up rich was something I usually did behind closed doors. Guiltily, I turned to Stephanie. "Sorry."

She smiled at me with sympathy. And I realized it was for more than one reason. She was sorry, too. This was not going to work out.

****

"This is really all your fault," I said, pointing at

Hayden.

He laughed. I gazed at his silhouette in the dark. We were standing at his car, both leaned up against it. Stephanie had left after the date, and we were debriefing in the parking lot.

"I'm sure it is," he admitted.

"It's because you intimidate women."

This seemed to surprise him. "Me?" He pointed at his chest. "Intimidating?"

"Yes. Absolutely."

"How?" he asked, his voice dripping with disbelief.

"Well, for starters, even in a suit, you can see this." I put my hand on his bicep and squeezed. Though I doubted he even felt it. The thing was massive. My tiny hand didn't fit all the way around it. I looked down at his thighs. "And one of your legs is the size of my entire body."

He looked down at me in the shadows. "You are very tiny," he agreed.

Tiny was not exactly the word I would use, maybe "compact." But the bottom line was Hayden, like most people, towered over me. Unlike most people, his body was thick with muscle that made even my curves look diminutive beside them.

"Yeah, well, you are freaking ripped."

"Thank you."

"How much time do you spend working out anyway?"

He shrugged one of his toned shoulders. "Not as much as I'd like these days. But for a while, bodybuilding was a pretty big hobby for me."

"Well, it shows," I complained.

"And that's intimidating?"

"Hell, yes. Women are always critical of our bodies. We are intimidated by a freaking sculpture of David as our date."

"That's rich coming from you," he said.

I bit my lip. I could have asked him what that meant. What was he saying? But I didn't. "The point is, between that, your position as a young CEO of a major corporation, and of course, the money—"

He turned his body toward me. "What is your hang up with the money, Chuck?"

"Well, Bobby, I don't like rich dudes."

"Just dudes?"

"What?"

"Well, I noticed that you are friends with some rich women. There's Grace, she's loaded. Candace has a great job. She makes a killing working for me at the company. Some people would call her rich. And you seem to get along with my sister pretty damn well. And, as you know, she has a trust fund and a share of the company profits just like me."

"Fine. Yeah. It's just dudes. You wanna drop me off at the BART? I need to get home."

"I'll drive you home. But first, I want to know about this rich-guy thing."

I didn't want him to drive me home. I didn't want him to see the shithole apartment in the bad part of town where I lived. I wanted that even less than I wanted to tell him about my past. So I negotiated.

"I'll tell you if you drop me off at the BART."

He seemed to chew on this for a minute. Then he nodded.

I let out a deep, shaky breath. "Okay. I dated a rich kid in high school. I thought I was madly in love with him. I was young and stupid and thought he was 'the one.' He came from a wealthy family, like yours. The only reason he was in public school was because he kept getting kicked out of the private ones."

"A bad boy, eh?"

"I always did like them that way," I said in a sultry voice. "Anyway, we were hot and heavy for *three fucking years*. I gave that prick my virginity, even. Then, after graduation, he dumped me. Like that." I snapped my fingers. "All because his parents thought I wasn't good enough for him. Me, a poor girl living in a shitty apartment with her single mom on the wrong side of town, I wasn't good enough for his rich ass."

"He broke your heart," Hayden said, his voice low.

I waved my hand dismissively. "He was an asshole."

"Agreed," he said. "And a moron."

"Whatever." I turned and tugged at the door handle. Hayden moved, and the door swung open. I pulled myself inside. "Take me to the BART station," I demanded, before slamming the car door.

****

I raced into the office and made it to my desk by eight fifty-nine. I prided myself on not being late. But early was definitely not my thing either. I threw my purse into the middle drawer of my desk and booted up my computer.

I glanced down at myself. I'd managed to put together a decent outfit despite my rush. I was wearing a deep crimson wrap dress that fell just above my knees and a pair of brown ballet slipper flats. I didn't mess around with tights. I hated them. And I didn't bother with tummy tuckers either. Instead, I tended to choose clothes that draped gracefully over my ample breasts, bigger-than-necessary-middle, and round hips. I'd done a good job this morning.

I had not, however, done a very good job with my hands. I looked at the remains of paint on my fingers and the swipe of blue across my palm. I'd gotten on a painting bender last night. And after a few hours of fitful sleep, I'd woken up and started again. I'd barely been able to pull myself away to get to work.

The worst part was the painting I'd been working wasn't just any scene, it illustrated Hayden's office. And, despite the fact that I rarely featured people prominently in my paintings, this one featured a man, a large, handsome man sitting casually on his desk.

My cheeks burned just thinking about it. Nervously, I peeked at Hayden's office door. It stood open just a crack. That's how he usually left it unless he was in a meeting. But I couldn't see him at his desk. I rolled my chair closer and peered through the crack like a thief. Hayden's chair sat empty.

That was strange. Hayden always beat me to the office. In fact, I suspected he arrived at insane hours these days. One of the other secretaries told me he was always there when she arrived at seven.

Another ten minutes passed before Hayden appeared in front of my desk. I looked him up and down. He looked rumpled and out of sorts. "What happened to you?"

He pulled his messenger bag off his shoulder and rested it on my desk. I loved that he carried that thing. Any other CEO would have a respectable briefcase. But in some ways Hayden was still the young playboy who'd been thrown into a job he wasn't ready for. Most of the time he never gave that away from his appearance. He wore expensive suits and shined shoes. But that dark green canvas bag, it was a nod to who was hiding beneath.

"Nothing happened to me," he said defensively. "I met up with my brother is all."

I was surprised, and happy, to hear this. I knew he and Jack used to have a standing appointment once a week just to have a coffee and catch up. But Hayden had canceled for the past few weeks, always having other meetings or deadlines.

I'd always wished I had siblings. And I envied the Morrisons for that, especially Chelsea. She had these two big brothers to harass her and take care of her. No one had ever looked out for me like that.

I smiled at him. "Oh yeah? That's cool then."

He took a seat in the chair opposite me. It was rarely used. Most people only stopped in front of my desk long enough to ask to see Hayden or to make an appointment. When Hayden and I worked together, we usually sat in his office. He had a big overstuffed chair in there for me to curl up in.

My guest chair, however, totally sucked. I chuckled as discomfort registered on his face.

"Jesus. Is your chair this shitty, too?" He examined the leather desk chair I was perched in.

I laughed. "No. But I do prefer the one in your office."

He stood. "Okay. Come on in, will you? We need to talk."

I followed him and shut the door behind me before taking my seat across from him.

He leaned forward, his arms resting on his desk. "I

think we should give up."

At first, I didn't understand what he was saying. Give up what? But then I realized what he meant. Last night was his last straw. "You mean the dating. Come on, Bobby. You've barely given it a chance," I argued.

"I've had three dates. Each one was a new kind of disaster. This blind date thing, it just isn't for me. Face it. I am not going to find a wife this way."

"You can't give up," I pleaded. Panic was starting to set in.

He leaned back and regarded me, folding his arms across his chest. "Why not?" He didn't ask the question casually, or the way a petulant child would. He asked like a man who was genuinely curious about the answer.

"I—I need the money."

Hayden let out a deep breath. "I can just loan you—"

I held my hand up. "No." Heat rose up my spine. I was certain my chest and neck had turned a dark pink color visible on my bronze skin. "I can't do that. I need to *earn* it." I knew I sounded desperate. And Hayden could hear it, too.

"Okay," he said soothingly. He unfolded his arms and leaned toward me again. "But you gotta tell me why you need the money so badly."

I bit my lip and considered that. I did not want to give that information up. But I wasn't in a position to keep my secrets, not anymore. My situation was precarious enough. I couldn't afford to have Hayden pull out.

I ran a hand across my face and then fisted that hand in the other, both twisted together in my lap.

"Okay. I'll tell you."

Hayden stared at me, the interest clear in his eyes, eyes that looked like the sky just after a storm. I gazed past him, out the window at his back, as I told him my dirty little secret.

"I was dating this guy, Franco. He was an artist, too. A sculptor. And he didn't have a place to stay. So, um, he was staying with me. We weren't together long. A couple of weeks. It wasn't…It wasn't serious. Just, you know, two artists, with a common attraction." I shrugged. This was so hard to admit, my stupidity, my shame. "He ran off one day and…and he took everything with him."

I sat and stared out the window for a long beat.

"What do you mean, everything?" Hayden asked.

I looked down at my hands. I used my fingernail to work at the slash of paint on my palm. "My money, some electronics, some art, my debit card. He, um, drained the account, then left town…everything."

Hayden was quiet for so long, I eventually looked up at him.

What I feared seeing in his eyes was pity. Instead they showed his anger and indignation. They reflected my pain and empathy. It was too much.

I stood. "So that's the story. I need the money to keep my apartment. And I lost my studio space because I got behind on the rent. I don't really have room at my place to work…and…and I need to get the studio space back. That's what the fifteen grand is for. It will pay my back rent, insurance, and a few more months forward. It will get me on my feet and tide me over until I can…" I trailed off. I was just rambling pointlessly now.

I straightened my dress and walked to the door. I

turned, my hand on the knob. Hayden was still sitting there at his desk, silent and concerned.

"So, can we keep our deal?" I asked. I tried to sound detached, to sound confident and angry, like I hadn't just opened up my wounds for him to see.

"Yes," he said softly.

I turned and walked out the door.

Chapter 7

One month and two weeks ago

My stomach twisted into knots as Candace pulled out her credit card. I wanted to rip it away from her and stop this whole thing. She slid the card into the reader, and we waited until it flashed *approved*. Neither of us spoke as the woman produced some papers to sign, followed by a key.

Candace didn't reach for the key, so I did. It practically burned my hand as I grasped it. Then we walked out to the rental truck together.

Candace eyed the truck. "I know we are both strong and capable, Meg. But I wish you'd let me get Jack to help."

I rolled the top of the truck up and looked at the artwork stacked in the back. My stomach threatened to give up the coffee and bagel I'd had for breakfast. This was all bad enough, without a bigger audience. I shook my head, trying to keep the tears at bay.

Candace put a hand on my back and rubbed gently. "It'll be okay, Meg."

I wished I could believe that. But it was hard. At thirty-two years old, I'd had everything right where I needed it. I had finally been making enough money from my art that I had my own apartment—no roommate—for the first time ever. I had a studio that allowed me to make and store art that could be shown and sold. I had been truly on my feet for first time.

And then I'd gone and blown it.

I didn't know why I was attracted to men who used me. Candace had always believed it was because I knew they were temporary and that made them safe. She claimed I was scared to death of a man that might be permanent. Maybe she was right. But it didn't matter now. That attraction for a hopeless, selfish loser had led me to utter ruin.

"I think this will work for the short term," Candace said, as she climbed into the back of the truck. "I mean, the unit is climate controlled, and there's enough space in there for us to place these along the walls and not have to stack too much."

It *was* a good temporary solution. After I'd gone in arrears on my studio, they had threatened to throw all my stuff out on the street if I didn't come get it. My tiny one-room apartment was already bursting at the seams, especially since I was now painting in what used to be my living room.

I had to have a place to put this stuff. I only wished I hadn't had to rely on Candace to put down the deposit and the first three months' rent.

"I swear I will pay you back soon," I said.

Candace sighed. "You know I don't care about that. I only care about you," she said for the millionth time today. "I wish you would believe that."

It wasn't that I didn't believe Candace cared about me. It was just so hard for me to accept that anyone would *take care* of me. Candace was the most trustworthy person I'd ever met. But in my life, that didn't mean anything. From my mother to every man who'd ever disappeared, no one had ever really meant it when they said they would stay. So I relied on only one person, ever—me.

We transferred my artwork from the truck to the storage unit. We mostly talked about where to put things and how to arrange the small room. When we were done, we buttoned everything up and got into the cab of the truck. I drove us back toward the truck rental place where we'd left Candace's car.

"Did you call the cops?" she asked when we were trapped in the vehicle together.

Damn. I did not want to lie to Candace. She loved me. And she believed I was a victim of a crime. She'd been relentless about me reporting Franco to the police. But I wasn't a victim. Not in the way Candace believed. I had let Franco into my apartment, into my life, and into my bed. I'd barely known him. I had no reason to trust him. In fact, I had chosen to hit on him precisely because he was the kind of man I *couldn't* trust. This was my own damn fault.

"Hmmm," I said, noncommittal.

She let out a huge breath and slumped into the seat beside me. She knew I wasn't going to do it.

"Hayden should be paying me big soon," I said to change the subject. "Then I'll get new studio space, and we can do this all over again. Maybe I'll even let Jack help."

Candace rolled her head to look at me. "How's that going with Hayden, anyway?"

"He's not so bad to work for, you know."

She chuckled. "I *do* know."

Of course she did. Candace worked for Hayden, too, though we rarely saw each other at the office. She headed up her own department, and her office was on a different floor, so we were only together at big meetings where I was sitting beside Hayden, taking notes. We did sneak off for lunch once in a while. But we usually spent that time talking about her baby, Sandy, the antics of her husband, Jack, or my art.

"He's completely capable of not only running the company, but taking it into the new era," I said confidently.

"I agree."

"But he doesn't believe that." As I said it I wondered if I was giving something away.

"I know," Candace said. "He is such a contradiction. He carries himself with this swagger. But deep down, he's a scared middle child, living in the shadow of his dad, his big brother, even his little sister."

"Do you think anyone else at the company knows?"

"That Hayden has insecurities about his position? No. He excels at showing a good front."

I couldn't agree more. I had discovered over the last few weeks Hayden was a completely different person beneath his shiny veneer. He was vulnerable and insecure. He was also generous. He'd given me everything I'd asked him for. And would give me more if I'd let him.

"How's the 'finding Hayden a wife' thing going?"

I laughed. "So far, *no bueno*. But I think everything is going to change tonight."

"Oh yeah? You have a big date lined up for him?"

I nodded. "Do you remember Jasmine Trudeau?"

"Um." She tapped her forefinger against her chin.

"The Trudeaus run that gallery in the North Bay you did a show at last year, right?"

"Yes. She's the daughter."

Candace furrowed her brow. "Isn't she kind of young?"

"She's young. But I think that's actually what Hayden needs."

"And why's that?"

"Hayden spent the first twenty-nine years of his life as a carefree playboy," I explained. "And now he's under all this pressure. He's doing a hell of a lot of adulting. He needs someone who can remind him to have fun every once in a while."

Somewhere along this crazy ride, I'd gone from caring primarily about making sure I got that check at the end to caring about what kind of person Hayden would end up with. I wanted him to be happy.

"I agree. He needs someone like you."

I nearly choked. "What?"

"You know, someone who lives life to the fullest," she explained. "I know you're having a hard time right now, Meg, but it will pass. The thing I've always admired most about you is that you never fail to live life on your terms."

I swallowed hard. "Thank you, sweetie. But what's that got to do with Hayden?"

"He needs someone like that, especially now. He has to live up to other people's expectations. And while he's perfectly capable of doing that, he could definitely use a woman in his life who reminds him, he also needs to live up to his *own* expectations."

"I am not following."

She laughed. "Too lawyery?"

"Yes. What the hell are you saying?" I asked, scared shitless of what it all really meant. Me and Hayden? Why had she said that?

"I mean, he needs to have fun once in a while," she said, parroting my words from a few minutes ago.

"I am not the only 'fun woman' around, you know."

"Of course not." She grinned. "Wow. I guess I hit a nerve. I thought Hayden was growing on you."

"He is," I admitted. "But not *that* much."

She laughed again. "Of course not."

****

I went back to work after settling my affairs at the storage unit. It was Friday, and Candace had taken the whole day off, so she left to pick up Sandy from her parents' house and spend the afternoon with her walking in the redwoods.

I was wishing I'd taken her up on the offer to join them as I walked down the main hallway that connected the break room to the elevator banks. I'd dropped off the leftovers from my lunch with Candace in the communal refrigerator and was headed back up to my desk to check e-mails.

Hayden was out of the office at a meeting. He probably wouldn't be back until almost four. And apparently, his biggest critic was taking advantage of the boss's absence. Jacob Wheeler was holding court in the hallway. His audience consisted of two members of his staff and a VP I recognized, but I didn't know his name or title.

"Look, he's got Phoebe replacing me. You guys will have to work extra hard to make up for her incompetence. But the truth is, that's nothing compared to what every one of the execs at this place has to do every day to make up for *his* incompetence. I'm telling you, Hayden is going to run this place into the ground."

I stopped behind him and examined the faces of the people he was talking to. Two of them were clearly skeptical. The third had spotted me and had a look of shock on her face. It made Jacob turn around.

"You little gossip queen," I said as he pierced me with his beady eyes. "You believe all this crap?" His audience squirmed on their feet, distinctly uncomfortable. "Can't you see through this guy's sour grapes?"

"Stay out of it," he grumbled.

"Why should she?" I turned to see a new face standing beside me. Thomas Green, one of the execs Jacob had just been talking about, stood almost a foot shorter than Jacob, but he carried himself with a sense of indignation that never went unnoticed. He spoke through thin, hard lips. "You've really become toxic, Jacob. This place is thriving and you know it."

Without any further discussion, Thomas stalked away. The rest of the gawkers abruptly departed as well, leaving me and Jacob staring each other down.

He leaned toward me. "I'm here for a little while yet, sweetie," he said menacingly. "And I intend to make that little shit's life as hard as possible for as long as I can. And there is nothing you can do about it."

"Really?" I stroked my chin as if I were thinking hard. "Because I got a call the other day for Hayden. It was a guy by the name of Gene Hennings. Does that ring a bell?"

His eyes grew wide, and I could see that I'd affected him.

"Gene wanted to talk to Hayden about you being fit for a position as CEO at Hennings and Hathaway. And Hayden was really nice. He said all kinds of great things about you. But you know, I still have Gene's phone number. And I think he might like to know about your behavior…" I let it sit there, while he took heavy breaths.

"Why would he believe you?" he asked, his voice thick.

"He's golfing buddies with my old boss, Rick Hoffman. You've heard of him, right?"

His eyes widened.

"Rick just loves me." I pulled my phone up in front of my face and scrolled through until I found Rick's cell phone number, then I tilted the screen so that Jacob could see it. I knew how this guy thought. As a hardened chauvinist, he believed that women only advanced in business by getting down on their knees. So I played on that. I cocked my hip out and put on a sultry face. "He would do just about anything for me."

"I got it," he nearly shouted. "I'll keep my mouth shut." He turned away from me as he capitulated.

"Not good enough," I said, folding my arms over my chest. "You should take that early retirement."

He grunted.

"Think about it," I said airily as I walked away, leaving him devastated in the hallway.

For the first time since I'd asked Hayden for a job at the rehearsal dinner, I felt like I'd finally paid him back in some small measure for all the things he'd done for me.

****

I hadn't thought about the implications when I'd

gone back to Hayden's place for a drink after his date with Jasmine. We'd both been so pleased that the date had gone well, that when Hayden suggested we walk to his condo, which was only a few blocks from the restaurant, I'd agreed. But as I walked into the high-rise and followed Hayden onto the secure elevator, I started to hedge.

Hayden ran a card through a reader and pushed a button before turning to me. "You done good, Chuck."

"Yeah, she's great, right?"

We'd gone to meet Jasmine straight from work, so Hayden was still in his suit. He looked hot as hell. And the effect was only increased as he loosened his tie. "I have to tell you. I thought you were nuts when she first showed up. She's pretty young."

I nodded. "She's twenty-two. But I don't think you should get hung up on that."

"I won't," he said casually.

"So, you've dated younger women before?"

He shrugged. "Sure, maybe not that much younger than me, but it's not a deal breaker."

The door to the elevator opened up directly into Hayden's penthouse, which was all the way at the top of the massive high-rise. He stepped out, and I followed him through a stark foyer and into the living room.

The living room alone was twice the size of my apartment. On one end, an open kitchen featured a marble-topped bar with tall stools all the way around. On the far side of the kitchen was a breakfast nook, but instead of a nice wooden dining set, the space was dominated by a foosball table.

The main area was furnished with a set of black leather couches and chairs along with a glass coffee table. The center of the room featured a massive entertainment center complete with a huge television and game console.

Directly opposite the elevator, sliding glass doors opened to a balcony. Beyond that was a short hallway I presumed led to a bathroom and at least two or three bedrooms.

The decorations were exactly what I would expect them to be in this rich boy's bachelor pad. A handful of pictures hung on the wall, mostly of him and his frat buddies. A fuzzy blanket draped over the back of the couch featured a pin-up girl design. There were no curtains, just white blinds. Aside from the photos and the pin-up girl, no color penetrated the space. Everything was in blacks, whites, and greys.

I absolutely hated it.

I turned my head at Hayden's laugh. "What?"

"You should see your face. My apartment disgusts you."

I shrugged. "It could use some work."

"I tell you what. I'll go get us something to drink, and you go out on the balcony. You might like it better from there."

I dropped my purse on his couch, just beneath the winking eye of the leggy girl on the blanket, and headed for the sliding door. As soon as I stepped out into the night, I knew that Hayden was right. This was breathtaking.

We were at least thirty stories above the street. From up there, I could see out across the Bay to the twinkling lights of Oakland, the graceful arch of the bridge, and the lines ripped through the water indicating the paths of ships.

The moon was almost full, and it left a soft bluish glow across the balcony. I stepped up to the railing and looked over. The night was still and warm, and I was completely comfortable in my dress and sandals and entirely enthralled with my surroundings.

I was nearly lost in my daydreams of being able to paint on a balcony like this, but not quite, because I was hyperaware of Hayden as he slid the door open and stepped out to join me.

He didn't speak as he moved to stand beside me. He had ditched the jacket and tie. The top two buttons on his white dress shirt were popped open, and his feet were bare. Heat rose up on my chest and neck. There was no denying that he was incredibly hot.

"Wine?" He held a glass out for me.

I took it and raised an eyebrow. "I didn't figure you for a wine drinker, Bobby."

He took a sip from his own glass. "Why not?"

"I thought frat boys preferred beer."

"I'm not a frat boy," he said stoically.

"You're not?"

"No."

I had been absolutely certain that was a trait of his. I cocked my head to one side. "Why not?"

"Wasn't my thing."

I turned around and faced the apartment. "I saw those pictures in there," I said, gesturing to the living room. "Those sure looked like frat-boy pictures to me."

I remembered the dudes with arms around one another, sneered lips facing the camera.

"Nah, just buddies. Some from boarding school, some from college. There's a couple pictures of my family in there, too, you know."

"So you like wine," I conceded.

He shrugged. "It's all right. To be honest, I keep it in the house because women tend to like wine." He wiggled his eyebrows.

"There's my playboy," I said, reaching up and grasping his chin.

"I'm not really the man whore you think I am, you know." He took a leisurely sip of his wine. "At least not anymore. Shit, I haven't had a girlfriend since I started that MBA program over two years ago."

"Who said anything about a girlfriend?" I teased. "I was thinking about you getting laid. Bringing girls back to your bachelor pad. You get the wine out, you say a few romantic things. You end up in the bedroom where there just happens to be a giant box of condoms conveniently placed in the bedside table."

He laughed. "I am not the player you think I am. I really do relationships. You're wrong about the seduction scene. I'm just not that smooth."

"Yes, you are," I blurted out. Because even though I hated rich boys and their games, I could totally see myself getting caught in this spider's trap.

He chuckled and leaned toward me. "You're right about the condoms, though. Maybe it's wishful thinking, but I *do* keep them in the bedside table."

His voice was low and his breath fanned over my ear as he confessed. It made me shiver. And I knew I had to make my escape.

"I'm glad the date went well. I need to head out." I slunk back to the door, which Hayden had left open, and made my way over the threshold.

It was strange walking back into the well-lit room after being on the dark balcony.

My feet were heavy as I made my way over to the bar. When I got there, I set down my half-empty glass of wine. I could feel Hayden right behind me. He placed his own glass down and leaned toward me.

"Don't go. Please," he said softly.

Chapter 8

I whirled around and found him to be even closer than I'd thought. He was right there in front of me, so big he practically engulfed me in his space. Unable to resist any longer, I placed my hands right on those massive pecs that sat, tempting me, at eye level. I let out a small moan of satisfaction when I found them to be just as hard and sculpted as I'd suspected.

I looked up at Hayden. His head was bent and he was watching me intently. "This is a bad idea." But I didn't move away. If anything I swayed closer.

"Probably." He brought his hand up to cup the back of my head and leaned closer.

I went up on my toes to reach for him. "I should probably go," I whispered.

"I wish you wouldn't."

Then our mouths met. And he was such an intoxicating combination of hard and soft, I couldn't help but part my lips and let him in. He took advantage, sweeping his tongue along mine.

A strange noise escaped my throat. Both of his hands went to my waist, and suddenly, my feet left the floor. The smooth, round surface of a barstool supported my ass. My sandals slipped off my feet as they swung beneath me.

In my haze, I recognized the advantage of this new position. Bobby and I were level now. I threw my arms around his neck and my legs around his waist, pulling him tight against me. I could feel his erection bumping up against the bottom of my thigh as he moaned deep in his throat. It was the most delicious sound I'd ever heard.

I knew I wasn't leaving. I knew I wasn't getting out of my boss's apartment without this whole thing turning into a raucous disaster. I decided if that was going to be the case, I would get exactly what I wanted.

I pushed on Bobby's chest. Reluctantly, he pulled away from our kiss and looked at me, a hint of regret in his eyes. It quickly turned to surprise when I said, "Take it off, Bobby," gesturing with my chin to his shirt.

He cocked his head to one side and regarded me with amusement.

"I mean it. I've been watching that work of art walk around in suits, and once, a T-shirt, God help me. And now I want you to unwrap that present, baby."

He immediately started untucking the shirt from his waistband. "You're really hot when you get all alpha, Chuck."

My eyes followed his fingers as they worked the buttons on his shirt. As each one was released, it exposed more of the landscape of him, hard muscle, ridged dips, and curves.

There was a moment where I had to call on all my patience while he worked at his cufflinks. But then he slid the expensive fabric down his arms and threw the garment to the ground.

I was still taking in the glory of him and thinking about how it would be to paint his magnificence, when he spoke. "My turn." His voice was rough and heavy.

Without looking away from him, I yanked the base of my dress from where it was trapped between the stool and my butt. Once it was free, I pulled it up my body and off in one quick movement, depositing it on the counter beside me.

I heard Bobby suck in a breath. Then his hands were on me. They started, parallel to one another, at my hips, then moved slowly upward, caressing the skin that was exposed between my panties and my bra. Then his left hand flipped over, and slowly, he ran the back of his index finger over the curve of my breast, across my nipple, and up to the skin above the seam.

"So beautiful," he whispered.

His right hand moved around behind my back and headed straight for the clasp on my bra. I grabbed his forearm and pulled it away. Of course, he was a thousand times stronger than me, but I was able to move him with the mere touch of my hand.

"Oh, no," I said, my tone teasing. "It's my turn. I want to see more." I nodded my head toward his pants.

He smiled, and without moving any farther away, unbuckled his belt, pulling it swiftly through the loops and tossing it on the floor. Then his hands went to the button of his slacks and made quick work of it and the zipper.

In one fluid movement, he pulled down his pants and boxer shorts, kicking them off and leaving him standing in front of me completely naked.

My hands went to his hard, thick thighs, while my eyes went to the organ jutting out at me above them. "I want to paint you," I mumbled.

Bobby didn't seem to hear me. He was single-minded. "Now," he breathed, his hands going back around to my bra clasp. With a single movement, he unhooked it.

My curves were ample, and my breasts heavy. The bra immediately dislodged itself and fell forward. With a simple swipe of his thumb, Bobby knocked it off my shoulders. I took my hands off him long enough to pull it all the way down and deposit it on top of my dress.

Bobby turned me on the stool so my back was to the counter. Then he lowered his head and licked my right nipple. I fell back onto the counter with a moan.

"Those are super sensitive," I breathed, clinging to his muscle-bound back.

This only seemed to encourage him. He increased the pressure of his lips, the flick of his tongue. I writhed and groaned beneath him. When I thought I would finally die, he moved to the other breast and began the perfect torture all over again.

I was a mass of nerves and pleasure when Bobby finally fell to his knees in front of me. He hooked his thumbs beneath the sides of my panties and tugged. I lifted my ass to help him extract them. And then they were gone.

Bobby sat back on his heels, hands on my thighs, holding them apart, and he stared, right there, at my sex. No one had ever done that before—just stared, admiring my most private of places. That's exactly what Bobby did. Minutes ticked by as he gazed at me, licking his lips, his breathing labored.

Watching him made something deep in my core quiver. "Bobby," I whispered.

Almost as if he'd forgotten himself, he snapped forward, his tongue jutting out to taste me. I threw my head back on a long, keening moan.

But it was only the beginning. Bobby licked and sucked until my orgasm crashed into me like a full speed train. I screamed and cried out in ecstasy and tried to convince him I was done.

But *he* wasn't.

After Bobby had made me come three times and my legs were shaking, my stomach rolling, my brow sweating, he finally stood. He kissed me tenderly. And I could taste my arousal on his tongue and feel his against my thigh.

"You really have that box of condoms in your bedroom?" I asked, out of breath.

He nodded.

"Go get one," I commanded.

He didn't wait for me to ask twice. I sat there, naked and spread-eagle on that stool, watching his perfect body cross the room. But once he was out of sight, I instantly regretted letting him go.

I stood up on shaky legs and began to make my way across the living room. It was as if I was chasing my prey, only it was me who was wounded and struggling. I rounded the couch and headed for the hallway when Bobby emerged.

He already had the condom on, and I looked down at it, completely distracted from my journey across the apartment. Without a single word, Bobby leaned over and scooped me up into his arms. He carried me, one arm behind my shoulders and the other under my knees.

I was small but not light. Despite that, Bobby, whose muscles were beyond anything I'd ever seen up close and personal, carried me as if I weighed no more than a sack of flour. He took me down the hall and through a doorway.

I didn't see much of my surroundings except the bed. It had a headboard, though I couldn't have said if it was wood or metal, and the blanket on top was colorful. That was all I saw before my head hit the pillow and Bobby's body covered mine.

He kissed me, deep and lovely. I put both of my hands firmly on that toned ass and pulled him to me. Bobby surged inside me—big, full, and hard as a rock. I broke my mouth away from his kiss to cry out an inarticulate celebration. Bobby groaned, then buried his face in my shoulder as he started to move.

It had been a long time since I'd had sex missionary style. I'd always considered it to be too tame. But as I pumped my hips to meet Bobby's rhythm, I decided I was completely wrong about this.

When yet another orgasm threatened to consume me, I swirled my hips and clenched. "Bobby, please," I whispered.

He moved, frantic and urgent. "Come for me, baby," he breathed. Then he shifted his head to take my mouth in a kiss.

As his tongue tangled with mine and his hips pumped, I reached my climax. Once I let go, Bobby followed right behind, his lips ravaging mine, a moan vibrating through us both.

Bobby collapsed beside me, one arm draped across my waist, his lips resting on my shoulder. For a long moment, we both just lay there, breathing heavily. Then I felt the wetness of the condom at the outside of my thigh as Bobby's erection faded. I scooped it up and tied it in a knot.

Bobby mumbled, "There's a trashcan next to you."

I rolled over and glanced around. A wicker basket

with a liner sat beneath an antique side table. I tossed the condom into it, then looked up at the table. It was a beautiful piece.

"Where did you get this table?" I asked.

"That antique fair they have once a month on Alameda."

I turned my head and took in the dark stain on the headboard which matched the color of the table perfectly. Then I popped up in the bed when my eyes caught a glimpse of what was hanging above the headboard. I stared up at it and blinked.

"This is mine," I said, my voice soft.

"Yeah. Don't you remember when I bought it?"

I turned to look at him. He was propped up on his elbow, studying me. "Yeah, but…I thought that was for the office."

"You didn't see it at the office, did you?"

"No, but I figured you just didn't really like it," I confessed. "So you didn't hang it up."

"Why would I buy a painting I don't like?" he asked genuinely.

I shrugged, suddenly feeling shy, not a sensation I was used to. "Even if you liked it, I wouldn't have guessed that you'd put it *here*."

It was an abstract painting of the Presidio. The foreground featured wildly colored blades of grass, large and dominating. The background featured tiny swaths of color representing people perched on the beach in the distance.

"It goes with my quilt," he said simply.

I examined the bed covering we were on. It was, in fact, a quilt, a handmade one by the looks of it. The patchwork of silk pieces in a variety of greens and blues had clearly been made with love and care.

"Where did you get it?" The awe I had as one artist admiring another's work came through in my voice.

"Sonya made it for me," he said, as if this instantly explained everything.

I gave him a questioning look.

Bobby took hold of my hand and toyed with my fingers. "She was our housekeeper when I was growing up. Well…housekeeper was what my mom called her. But in a lot ways, she was more like a nanny. She was an integral part of our lives all through my childhood."

"Where is she now?"

"She lives in an assisted-living facility in the North Bay. I go visit her every Sunday after I have brunch at my parents' house."

I was completely fascinated by this. "So…you and your siblings go?"

"No, just me. I mean, I think Chelsea's gone to visit a few times, and I know Jack calls and sends cards. But I go alone on Sundays. It's our time. She has kids of her own, too. But they don't come on Sundays."

"You're really close to her?"

"Yeah."

"Closer than Jack and Chelsea are to her?"

He nodded. Then he smiled. "I'm her favorite, always was. It's kind of nice. I am certain Sonya is the only person who ever considered me her favorite Morrison."

I looked into his blue eyes, and a thought spontaneously popped into my head. The Bobby I'd come to know, the one who had become my friend, the one who I'd just shared amazing sex with, he had somehow become *my* favorite Morrison, too.

I swung my legs off the bed and stood up. "I should get going."

Bobby frowned at me. "I don't suppose I can talk you into staying?"

I shook my head. I felt the overwhelming urge to flee. But I didn't want to seem ungrateful. After all, Bobby had given me the best evening I'd had in years. So I leaned over and gave him a quick kiss. "Not tonight."

I turned and walked out of his bedroom. It sat at the end of the hallway, and I quickly made my way down the corridor toward the center of the apartment, my bare feet slapping against the floors. When I caught sight of my clothes sitting on the kitchen counter, I practically ran to them.

I threw on my bra and dress, located my panties and shimmied them on under the dress, then slid my feet into my sandals. I turned to grab my purse from the couch and saw Bobby standing there. He was leaned up against the wall at the end of the hallway, wearing only a pair of boxer shorts.

"If you give me a minute to throw on some clothes, I'll drive you home," he said.

I had to step closer to him to retrieve my purse. I walked to the couch and threw the strap across my shoulder. "Nah. That's okay. I'll use my ride-share app."

His eyebrows scrunched up, and I could see I'd offended him.

"It's just…" Then the truth came flying out of my mouth. "I don't want you to see where I live." His frown grew deeper, and I scrambled to explain. "It's not like, I don't want you to know where I live. It's that…I'm ashamed of the shithole I live in, see?"

"Hmmm." His mouth curved in a modest smile. "Thank you for telling me the truth."

I nodded.

He walked across the room and over to where his pants lay on the floor. I stood there, frozen from curiosity, as he dug through them. My stomach clenched as I worked through the fear that he would pull out money for a cab. That would make me feel so cheap.

Instead, Bobby pulled out his cell phone. He pushed a button, and I heard it ringing through the speaker. "Hello, Mr. Morrison. What can I do for you?" a voice answered.

"Hi, Kyle. My friend is in need of a ride. Can you have the limo waiting out front?"

"Absolutely, Mr. Morrison."

He turned to me. "My solution," he said, presenting it as if it were a gift. And in a way it was.

"Thank you."

From across the room, he nodded. I walked to the door. With my hand on the knob, I turned to take one last look at him. "You are a very sexy man, Hayden."

"Right back atcha, Meg."

Chapter 9

My leg was shaking up and down beneath the table, but no one seemed to notice, thank God.

"Okay, here they are, ladies. The greatest burgers you've ever eaten," Henry said, placing a plate full of plump hamburgers in the center of the table.

"He is ridiculous about the grill," Chelsea said, gesturing with her head to the porch, where Henry had been laboring to cook us dinner.

"I am a master," Henry said, kissing her on the cheek, before taking his place at the table with us.

I had not been able to come up with a good excuse to cancel dinner at Chelsea and Henry's house on Saturday night. And normally, I wouldn't even dream of it. I enjoyed the hell out of the carefree newlyweds. I'd met Chelsea after her brother married my best friend, and we'd become fast friends. After she and Henry got together, we'd started a tradition of having dinner once a month, just the three of us.

The timing was terrible because I just so happened to have slept with Chelsea's other brother the night before. It was all I could think about.

"So Candace talked to Grace," Chelsea said, leaning over the table.

"Is she still in Rio?"

Chelsea nodded, grinning.

When Grace hadn't shown up for Henry and

Chelsea's wedding last month, we'd all panicked until we'd discovered that she'd fled to Rio and into the arms of Meno. Now we were all fascinated with what was happening thousands of miles away.

"And?"

"Apparently, she's been working at his restaurant."

"Grace, working at a restaurant?" I was floored. As far as I knew, Grace had never worked a day in her life.

Chelsea nodded enthusiastically. "Can you imagine?"

While we put together our burgers and passed around the salad, we speculated about whether or not there was a romantic element to what was going on between Meno and Grace.

"The guy is hot, though, I have to say," I opined.

Henry rolled his eyes, and Chelsea laughed. "Sore subject, Meg. Henry thought I slept with Meno once, before we were together. He was jealous as hell." She smiled lovingly at her husband. "It was cute."

"I'm glad you think so," he grumbled.

"You guys are freaking adorable," I said casually, before taking a bite of my burger.

After we spent a little bit of time enjoying Henry's masterpiece, Chelsea asked me, "How's your love life, Meg?"

I nearly choked on the beer I was sipping. I put the bottle down and tried to act casual. "Nothing exciting." God, I was a horrible person, because that was a huge lie. But what could I say? Your brother is the best lover I've ever had, and I had the opportunity to find that out last night? No, thank you.

"What about Hayden?" she asked.

My heart was literally pounding. I knew it was just

a coincidence that she'd asked those two questions in sequence, but I couldn't seem to gather myself up to answer.

"Yeah, aren't you working on finding him a wife?" Henry asked.

I let out my breath. "Yeah. I am actually."

"A wife for Hayden," Chelsea mused. "That's hard to picture."

I was intrigued. "Why's that?"

She shrugged. "I don't know. Hayden just…God, how do I say this without it sounding awful…I'll just say it. In my opinion, Hayden was too good for all the women he chose to be with."

"Really? Tell me about them." Before she could get too curious about why I was interested, I explained. "It will help me choose dates for him."

"Oh, I don't know," Chelsea said, "All of them were a little…one dimensional."

"Were they all like him…like you…?"

"Rich?" she asked, saving me.

I nodded.

"No. The only ones that came from wealthy families were the girls he dated after Jack had dated them. Man, for a while there, Hayden was all about Jack's leavings." She laughed. "That stopped in college though. Hayden went off to Florida and dated a few girls for quite a long stretch each. They were all regular middle-class women. But they didn't…I don't know. They weren't sharp and witty like Hayden. They were just kind of bland. It was like he was purposefully attracted to women like that."

"Really?" I said.

"Yeah. I remember I once asked him why he liked

women that weren't anywhere near as awesome as he is." After making that statement, she paused and took a bite of potato salad. I wanted to bat her upside the head.

"Well, how did he respond?" I asked impatiently.

She finished chewing and looked at me, remembering. "He kissed the top of my head and said, 'Oh, Chels. You just think I'm better than I am.' "

That matched exactly what I would expect from Bobby.

"Well, I fully intend to fix him up with women that *are* good enough for him," I said confidently.

Chelsea smiled. "I have complete faith in you, Meg."

My stomach sank as I wondered if I deserved that trust or not.

****

I spent the entire weekend dreading Monday. But I shouldn't have wasted my anxiety because Hayden treated me with the utmost respect and professionalism, just as he always had before I slept with him. When I brought him coffee that morning, he smiled kindly and thanked me profusely. When I sat with him in the meeting with the execs, he addressed me formally, but with gratitude and even a little reverence.

And even though I couldn't help but think about the amazing body hiding beneath his suit, he didn't seem the least bit affected by my sexiest work dress, a low cut pencil in deep red.

By six, I found myself still at my desk, having completely lost track of time as I ran over paranoid thoughts again and again in my head. I stood and marched into Hayden's office without any warning.

He sat forward in his large leather chair, elbows

planted on the desk, eyes glued to his computer screen. He had an appointment tonight, and I knew he was looking over the documents I'd sent him in preparation for it.

As my heels traveled over the thick carpeting at the threshold to his office, his head snapped up. "Meg. You're still here."

I didn't stop my forward motion as I pushed the door closed roughly. The knob clicked into place just as I arrived at his desk. He followed me with his gaze and turned in his chair as I moved around the hulking wooden furniture to stand beside him.

"Did you hear that Jacob took the early retirement after all?"

I had heard, and I was glad, but I could only manage a simple nod. I folded my arms across my chest. "We need to talk."

He leaned back in his leather desk chair, interlacing his fingers to support his head. "Okay," he said congenially.

"How many of your secretaries have you slept with?"

Hayden's hands shot out from behind his head and he leaned toward me. "Excuse me?"

"You are obviously practiced at this. And I'd like to know how practiced."

Anger burned in his eyes. "None," he said quickly. Then he swiveled in his chair and focused his attention back on the computer.

I turned and leaned my ass up against the top drawer of his desk, looking out the window at the city below us. "It's just that you are very good at separating business from pleasure, and I just thought...maybe...it was because…" I faded off. It sounded too stupid to continue. And I started to wonder if maybe I was on the wrong track. Instead of Hayden being a smarmy exec too good at seducing his secretaries, maybe this was about me wanting to know I was special, wanting to feel that I was so sexy he couldn't resist me.

A few tense minutes went by. I heard Hayden clicking his mouse. I took several deep breaths and stayed silent by his side. Finally, I turned and peered over his shoulder at the computer. He leaned back to give me a better view of the screen.

"These," he said, pointing at the pictures he'd pulled up, "are my past secretaries." There were three of them. Each one more beautiful than the last. They were young, thin, and well put together. "They were all single, and I didn't so much as make a pass at any of them."

My voice sounded small and far away. "Why not?"

Hayden turned his chair again so he faced me. He pulled on the back of my thighs. I lost my balance and landed on his lap. My dress rode up as my legs stretched around his to straddle his waist.

"Chuck," he said softly. And it didn't escape my notice that it was the first time all day he'd called me that. "I didn't sleep with you because you are my secretary. I slept with you because I am *extremely* attracted to you. And I treated you like I did today because, even though I know you are only here temporarily, I would like to keep you as my assistant for as long as possible. Why? Because you are very, very good at your job and I need you. And because it will be much easier to convince you to sleep with me again if you are close by. I figured if I managed to hide the fact that I've wanted to rip this dress off you all day long, I would have a better chance at keeping you from quitting." He cocked his head to one side. "Was I wrong?"

Completely floored and thoroughly turned on, I found it hard to breathe. So I just shook my head.

Bobby's gaze traveled from my face down my body, and it made me burn. "You are so gorgeous," he whispered. "And this dress…" He ran a hand up my thigh, pushing the bottom hem even higher. "It's been killing me all day."

I leaned forward and took his lips with my own. A thick groan escaped me as Bobby's thumb rubbed against my silk panties, asking to come in.

It only took a few clothing adjustments, the retrieval of a condom from Bobby's wallet, and a willingness to completely forget that we were at work, and Bobby was inside me.

I rode his lap with an abandon I'd forgotten I could feel. I certainly made noise, but I couldn't be entirely sure because my whole being focused intensely on the sounds coming from Bobby's throat. Low and deep, he murmured incoherent noises filled with desire and pleasure. His voice box became my instrument. A movement here, a caress there, and I could manipulate it, making my own music.

When we'd both climaxed and I collapsed on top of him, still straddling him in the chair, we kept kissing for a good long time. I finally pulled away.

I rested my forehead against Bobby's. "That was bad," I breathed.

He chuckled. "I so don't care."

"Not very CEO-like," I teased.

"I suppose that depends on the CEO."

"Touché."

"Come home with me tonight. I am begging you."

"And you are very cute when you beg," I said, pulling myself off his lap. "But I have things to do tonight." I straightened my dress and leaned down to pick up what remained of my panties, which, in a frantic moment of need, Bobby had used a pair of scissors from his desk to cut off me. "One of which is to make arrangements for your next date with Jasmine." I stood and pointed at him, my wrecked panties dangling from my hand. "And you have that dinner meeting with your uncle and the guy he wants you to hire to be his replacement in an hour."

He groaned. His uncle, the company's CFO, also planned to retire soon. It added additional stress to Hayden's already burdened shoulders. I hoped that if he could hire a good replacement, they would help him.

"Fuck," he said under his breath.

I chuckled. "I guess not."

He looked up at me, his eyes full of promise. "You could come over later. Kyle will let you in. Hell, it could be as late you want. Wake me up."

I couldn't help but smile at his enthusiasm. I loved the way Bobby wanted me. I shook my head, but I knew deep down that I'd be headed over there tonight.

****

On Wednesday afternoon, I sat at my desk editing a memo from Hayden to his execs when a pair of remarkable legs appeared in front of me. My gazed traveled upward to see my best friend staring down at me.

I had been avoiding Candace since Friday night.

I'd found every way possible to not be in her presence. After twenty years of friendship, I was certain she would see the sex I was having written all over my face.

It was silly, really. I mean, she'd never been able to tell that before. She'd never walked up to me, looked at my face, and accused me of getting laid. But then again, I'd never been so sexually satisfied in my life. Was it written all over me? Could she see it in the new brightness of my eyes or the involuntary curve of my lips which gave me an almost constant half-smile? If she asked, I didn't want to lie about it, but I certainly didn't want to tell her that I had spent the last few nights romping around her brother-in-law's massive king bed.

"Hi, Candace," I said casually.

"I feel like I haven't seen you in forever." She held out her arms. "Give me a hug."

I got up and rounded my desk. Candace was significantly taller than me and built like a freaking model. She enveloped me in a huge hug, and I squeezed her tight. I had missed her, too.

"So," she said, pulling back. "You're going to be mad at me."

"Why?"

"Hayden and I made an appointment by text this morning, and I forgot to tell you so you could put it in his calendar."

I shrugged. "I'm not that controlling a secretary. It's okay."

"Yeah, but it involves you, too."

Panic bubbled up in me. "Yeah?"

"Come on." She tilted her head toward Hayden's door.

I followed her into his office on pins and needles. I didn't know what was about to happen. Did she know about us? Hayden and I hadn't actually talked about whom we would or wouldn't tell. Perhaps he'd told Jack. Maybe Jack had told her, and she was here to confront us.

All this ran through my head as I sat down beside her on the little loveseat perpendicular to Hayden's desk. They talked casually, greeting one another while I waited, shaking in my boots.

Hayden moved his desk chair so that he sat closer to us. "So, what do you have in mind for my big brother's birthday?"

I let out a breath I didn't realize I was holding.

"Well, Sandy and I got him a new car. So I was thinking whatever we planned, we could incorporate the car," Candace said.

"You bought him a *car*?" I asked.

"Have you seen the death trap he drives around?" Candace threw her hands up in exasperation. "It's not safe. I won't let him put Sandy in it, and he says he can't afford a new one." She rolled her eyes. "And since I can't seem to convince my husband that my money is also his money—"

"Or to use the portion of the company profits that rightfully belong to him on himself instead of sinking every dime into charity," Hayden interjected with a proud smile.

"Exactly, so I have to get him the car for his birthday," Candace explained.

I knew all about Candace and Jack's squabbles over money, so I just smiled at her. "Good solution. He'll hate it."

"I know," she said, grinning. "All the more reason to make it a big deal so he can't whine in front of everyone."

"So, are we thinking big party or small shindig at Mom and Dad's?" Hayden asked.

"Big party!" Candace said enthusiastically. "We'll let him know about the party, but keep the car a surprise."

"Thank God we still have two months to plan it," I said.

"So are you both in? You'll help me?" Candace swiveled her head from side to side looking at us both.

"Of course," I said.

"Sure," Hayden agreed. "We'll get the place and the catering taken care of."

"Great. Chelsea and your mom are doing the guest list. I feel like I won't have much to do." Candace granted us a sly smile.

"You have the hardest part," Hayden told her. "You have to get him there. Jack hates his birthday."

"Yeah. Why is that?" she asked Hayden, cocking her head. "Do you know?"

Hayden leaned toward us conspiratorially. "When we were growing up, he always made a big deal out of Chelsea's and my birthday, but he practically hid out when his own rolled around. When we got older, Chelsea and I tried to make a big deal of his birthday, but it was too late. He was already soured on it."

"What happened? What do you mean 'it was too late?' "

"His birthday is in the beginning of September, so it always happened right after we got to boarding school. Mom and Dad were always busy getting us ready to go and forgot to celebrate it beforehand. When his birthday hit, school had just started and we weren't settled in yet. No one at school knew to make a big deal. I mean, Chelsea's is near Christmas and we celebrated when we were home for the holiday, and mine is in the summer. But Jack got screwed." He shrugged. "I think it was really hard on him, and then his birthday just became a bad memory."

"That is so sad," Candace said.

I nodded my head. "My mom was a pretty shitty parent, but at least she always did something for my birthday," I said, remembering the discount store-bought cake and dime-store gifts wrapped in newspaper.

"Once I was old enough to figure it out," Hayden explained. "I tried. I really did. One year, when Jack turned fifteen, I got all his friends together and we snuck him out of school and toilet-papered the headmaster's house."

I shook my head and clucked my tongue. "Bad boys." I couldn't help but smile at the thought of twelve-year-old Hayden organizing such a prank.

"That was nothing compared to the year he turned nineteen." He laughed to himself, remembering.

"What happened?" Candace asked.

"Oh no. I am not telling *you*, Candace. You can ask your husband about that one."

"Wait, wasn't he going to Stanford at that point?" I asked.

"Yep." Hayden grinned. "In fact, it was right before he dropped out and took off for Rio. I was at boarding school in So-Cal. I convinced this senior, an ex-girlfriend of Jack's, to drive me up to Stanford. That was a good year."

"So, it wasn't always so bad between you, then?" Candace asked, alluding to the well-known fact that Hayden and Jack hadn't gotten along from the beginning of high school until just a few years ago.

"We had exactly two times a year we had a truce, his birthday and mine. Every other day, including holidays, was the usual. But on those two days, we were golden. It was an unspoken thing. Weird, I guess," he said, sounding thoughtful.

"Yes, weird." Candace stood. "Well. I appreciate your help with his thirty-third birthday, and I'm glad you two get along better these days." She leaned over and kissed Hayden's cheek before heading to the door. "I'm going to go back to my office and get some work done now, before my boss gets mad." She winked at us both and walked out the door, closing it behind her.

I couldn't help but wonder what was happening inside Hayden's head just then. Years ago, when Candace had first started working for Hayden, he'd asked her out. And we all knew he'd harbored a crush on her for a long time after she and Jack got together. But no one had said anything about it recently.

Rather than go down that rabbit hole in my brain, I leaned forward and kissed Hayden's other cheek. "You are so much sweeter than you let on."

He captured my hands in his. "You think I'm sweet?"

"Sure," I said casually, not wanting to let on just how attractive I found it.

"You used to think I was an asshole."

"I was wrong," I said simply. Because it was true.

He leaned in for a kiss, but I leaned away. "We

need to settle something."

"Okay," he said hesitantly.

"When Candace first showed up here this afternoon, I thought she knew about us."

"I don't think so. Not unless you told her."

"No. I haven't. But I thought maybe you told Jack."

"No."

"Have you told anyone else?" I asked.

"No. Not yet. I mean, I guess I wasn't sure—"

"Good," I said, interrupting him. "I think, given that I am in the process of finding you a wife, and that I work for you, this…*thing*…that we have going on should just be our little secret."

"I suppose." His tone was noncommittal.

"So we're good with that?" I asked, hoping for a more secure promise.

"Sure, Chuck. We're good." He reached forward and wrapped his big hand around my waist. "If you come here and give me something to keep a secret about."

Chapter 10

One month and one week ago

I woke up to the sound of my alarm. On instinct, I fumbled for my phone on the nightstand and shut it off. I stretched, and my hands touched Bobby's headboard. I smiled as I remembered that during a particularly naughty moment last night my feet were pressed up against that wooden piece.

I rolled over and was instantly disappointed when I looked at the empty space in the bed beside me. I reached for the note, written on yellow legal paper and perched on Bobby's pillow. I unfolded it and read his messy scrawl.

Chuck—

I had an early meeting. You were too cute to wake up. See you at work.

—B

I left the note on the bedside table and picked up my phone as I crawled out of bed and made my way across the room. I'd started carrying a large bag in place of my purse so I could keep a change of clothes in it. The bag sat where I'd left it on top of Bobby's dresser, and beside it my clothes from the day before were neatly folded in a tidy stack.

Last night, those clothes had been strewn from the elevator to the bed as Bobby and I ravished each other upon walking inside. Bobby had collected them and left them in this neat little pile for me. I smiled to myself as I pulled a fresh pair of undies, bra, and cotton dress out of my bag, then went to the utility room to start up the steamer.

Half an hour later, showered and dressed, I made my way to the kitchen to find something to eat. After grabbing a cup of coffee from Bobby's fancy coffee maker and a bagel with cream cheese, I plopped down on a stool at the bar and looked at the gift Bobby left me.

Another piece of yellow legal paper held a note that lay unfolded and draped lazily over the laptop computer.

Chuck,

Before you argue, this is for me. You need to have a computer that you can use to check my calendar or edit my documents any time night or day...

That wasn't true. I could do both things easily on my phone.

So here's a computer for you. I want you to keep it and use it. And don't give me any shit about it.

Below his *B* was the computer's password. I opened the laptop. It was brand new, top of the line, and already charged up and turned on. I entered the password to unlock the screen. Shocked, I perused the computer's software and found that it had been pre-loaded with everything I could ever imagine needing, including several art programs.

I sat back and stared at it for a long time while I nibbled on my bagel. This was not about work. It was a gift. I fought the urge to immediately box it up and shove it at Bobby, insisting he return it.

I tried to work on being gracious. I would hurt him if I refused his gift. And really, there was no reason to do that. The gesture wasn't sinister. No strings or implied favors came with it. It didn't amount to anything more than Bobby wanting to take care of me.

And there it was again. My stomach-churning reaction to this gift was based on my own hang-ups. It wasn't Bobby's fault, and I decided I wouldn't punish him for it.

As I pushed aside my empty plate and pulled the computer closer to me, I thought about how I took care of Bobby, too. I really did organize his life on an everyday basis. I kept him always prepared for the demands of his job, and I stood up for him with creeps like Jacob.

I pulled up Hayden's calendar on my new computer and immediately felt slightly sick. Today's meetings were all normal, nothing out of the ordinary. But at the end of the day, after work, he would be meeting up with Jasmine again. "Date 2," I'd marked it.

It was my job to make sure this went well. By finding Hayden a wife, someone who could fulfill his needs as a CEO and provide a stable home life that would live up to his position, I was taking care of him.

I pushed aside the dark feeling that had taken over me when I spotted that calendar entry and turned to my phone. I jabbed out a quick text to Jasmine.

—Ready for tonight?—

—I can't wait. Are you coming, too?—

I probably shouldn't. I should let them be alone. But I really didn't want to.

—I think I should come just to make sure things go smoothly. I will disappear for date 3.—

—OK. You seem sure there will be a date 3.—

—I am. You like Hayden, don't you?—

—YES! He's smart and funny and super hot!—

—He is all of those things.—

—Do you think he likes me?—

—If he didn't, there wouldn't be a date 2. See you tonight.—

I set my phone aside and hung my head in my hands. What the hell was I doing?

****

I watched Hayden and Jasmine together as if I were seeing it all through a hazy window. They sat there, just a few feet away from me, but I might as well as have been separated by a physical barrier.

It wasn't my job to participate in this date. In fact, I should have left once I'd confirmed things were going well. But I couldn't seem to pry myself out of the third-wheel seat I occupied in the restaurant.

As I watched them, I tried to anticipate what Hayden would say next in the conversation. But I failed every single time. This wasn't my Bobby sitting here. Hayden, the playboy, the CEO, polished and self-confident, even a little cocky, ran this show. And I had to admit it was sexy as hell. In fact, Jasmine was eating it up. She leaned toward him, eyes wide, lips parted, a slight flush on her cheeks.

I, too, felt warm watching him. But it was less because of the man in front of me than it was the man I knew lived beneath Hayden's exterior—my Bobby.

Jasmine really was a good match for Hayden. Young and materialistic, she'd never had to mature by walking through the hard parts of life. Soft, polished, and shiny, she'd been raised with the poise and grace that comes easily with money. She could play the role of the CEO's wife perfectly.

She wouldn't hold Hayden's interest forever, though. For now, she was hot and sexy as well as smooth and accommodating. But no challenge lay in being with a woman like her. And deep down, they had little in common. It would be a temporary marriage, a few years perhaps. But it would accomplish Hayden's goals.

My eyelids felt twitchy and my butt uncomfortable on the seat as Hayden and Jasmine discussed the details for a weekend date I'd arranged. Lost in the sound of his voice, I got hit with the stark realization that I didn't have much time left with Bobby.

Soon the CEO would take over full time. He would have to for Hayden to survive his responsibilities. And with a woman like Jasmine at his side, it would only accelerate that process.

I made a mental bucket list for my remaining time, which I realized would be very short. Obviously, as much sex as possible sat at the top of the list. But there was more.

Honesty sat between Bobby and me like a beloved family dog. We always told each other the truth. It felt like a betrayal of that to hide where I lived from him. A person's apartment said so much about them. Hadn't I analyzed every object in Bobby's place in detail?

I decided to show Bobby my apartment, to open myself up to him. Of course that also meant he'd see my current art project. I chewed on my lip and wondered if that was a good idea or not. My gaze slid around the room and came to rest on Hayden. He stared at me, his concentration pinned on the lip between my teeth.

Jasmine said something and recalled his attention. As I sat there, a perverse spectator to this date, I decided that, with the little time I had left, I would give Bobby everything. It was terribly selfish. I wanted to do it for me. I wanted to carry the memories of our brief affair with me as I trudged through what was sure to be a lackluster love life for the next fifty or sixty years.

After Hayden and Jasmine made arrangements to drive down to a beachfront resort near Santa Cruz Friday morning, we walked Jasmine out to her car. We stood there in the cool, dark night, and she angled for a kiss. The body language was clear, unmistakable. Being shorter than Hayden, but taller than me, she got up on her toes, bringing her lips to his chin level. She put her hands on his upper arms. She tipped her head up.

Bobby's jaw ticked. He looked at her, but his energy was focused on me. I knew I needed to walk away. I needed to give them privacy. I shouldn't watch the man I planned to have wild sex with later kiss another woman.

But I couldn't walk away. I stood there, just feet away from them both, and willed him not to do it. Give me twenty-four more hours. Then he could kiss her all he wanted. But we were still on my time.

Hayden leaned down and whispered something in Jasmine's ear. Whatever it was, it appeased her. Her heels fell to the ground, and she smiled as he kissed her cheek. Then she turned to me and shook my hand, thanking me for connecting her and Hayden.

I felt like a fraud.

****

I watched Bobby closely as he took in my

apartment. In contrast to his sparsely decorated place, here every surface was covered. An already minuscule living quarters housing my overwhelming amount of personal shit had been overburdened with art supplies when I had to close my studio

Bobby's gaze went from one end of the single room to the other with no expression change. He could see it all, the tiny kitchen overflowing with hand-knitted towels and oven mitts, to the living room crammed with my painting gear and one tiny loveseat, to the bed, draped with a variety of crocheted afghans and dying, listless pillows.

I didn't have a headboard, just a plain mattress and box spring. I didn't have a television or computer because Franco had stolen them. I didn't have a color scheme, because everything I owned was either a gift or an art-fair special. My home swirled with a chaotic mix of colors and textures.

"You were right, Chuck. It does say a lot about you." He turned to me and smiled, one arm snaking around my waist.

"There's something else," I told him, moving away. I walked over to the easel that took up the space near the bed where the television had once been.

The large canvas I'd been working sat covered with a cloth. I'd hung it after finishing the painting, ashamed of what of I'd done and afraid of what it meant. But now, I yanked away the cloth and exposed it, exposed myself.

Bobby's face wore a thoughtful expression as he stepped forward to get a closer look.

"It's more realistic than what I usually paint," I said weakly. "And I haven't done a person like this since college. So…"

Bobby looked at his portrait. In it he sat leisurely on top of his desk. One leg reached the floor, while the other sat at an angle and dangled beneath him casually. His calm, almost neutral expression was betrayed by a hint of mischief in his bright blue eyes. The large windows of his office served as a backdrop showing the sun beating down on the city and the bay.

A long moment skated by us as he looked and I watched. Then he spoke, his voice so soft I barely heard him. "Is it me or Hayden?"

The question floored me. I hadn't realized that he understood the depths of my depravity. He *knew*. He knew that I saw him as two people, one to work for, one to have fun with and make love to.

We stared at each other. He waited for the answer, and I tried to climb over my shock. When I didn't speak, he took a step closer.

"Both," I finally confessed.

"Hmmm." He turned back to the painting.

"You are both in there. The suit and the office are Hayden. But the expression on your face, the mussed-up hair because you've been running your fingers through it, the way you're sitting on the desk, relaxed and carefree. That's my Bobby."

He didn't look at me. He continued to stare at the painting. And for once, I could not read him.

"What are you thinking?" I whispered, more to myself than to him.

His eyes met mine. "That I'm naked in this picture. Exposed."

It was true.

"And I would very much like *you* to be that way

right now." A sexy challenge shone in his eyes, and I could breathe again.

I threw the cloth I was still clutching in my hand to one side and stepped away from the painting, toward the bed. "Like this?" I lifted my dress to my waist.

He nodded. "All the way, sweetheart."

I grinned and pulled my dress off. Then I pulled my bra off and looped my thumbs in the sides of my panties. I paused. "These too?"

Bobby's eyes burned. "Hell, yes."

I shucked the panties off and kicked them to the side. Completely naked, I walked to the bed and sat down in the middle.

"Now you get to be the painting," Bobby said appreciatively.

I shivered. Never, never had I felt so desired, so sexy, so *wanted.* I lay down on the bed and closed my eyes, basking in his stare. I knew he was looking at me, every corner of me, every hidden tone, every secret curve.

Even with my eyes closed, I knew when Bobby began to shed his clothes. I concentrated on each sound. Cloth moved, buttons were forced through holes, shoes clunked on the cheap linoleum. The rip of the zipper made me shake with anticipation.

A few quick moments later, Bobby hovered over me, his skin against mine. He kissed my neck and whispered, "You are more beautiful than any work of art ever made, Chuck. You are perfection."

My eyes flew open, and my hands came up. I grasped onto him and pushed so he rolled over onto his back. Like a ravenous animal, I attacked his mouth while simultaneously moving to straddle his hips.

From this position, I could take in every tiny movement on Bobby's face as we made love. I controlled our speed and the depths with which we sank into one another. And I gave Bobby everything that was in my soul.

As soon as my orgasm had faded and I had wrung Bobby dry, a deep sense of loss overtook me. I climbed off him and lay face up beside him on the bed.

Bobby shifted so he could watch me. He ran one hand slowly along my side, from the bottom of my breast to my hip and back up again.

"Are you okay?" he asked softly.

I shook my head. I didn't want to see the concern in his eyes, so I kept my gaze focused on the ceiling. "That's it, Bobby. That was the last time. I'll just miss it, that's all."

He stayed quiet for a long moment. The steady in and out of his breathing was so comforting it ached. "It doesn't have to be."

"It does. You and Jasmine are good together. This weekend is a getaway date. You'll have sex. You'll get close. You'll move toward where you need to be. It's not my job to get in the way of that. In fact, just the opposite."

"What if I want to sleep with you more than I want to go to the next level with Jasmine?"

This had me jumping out of the bed. I stood beside it, glaring down at him. "No way, Bobby. No! You can't do that. You can't throw away the opportunity for a wife that you need for a little more fuck time with me."

A fierce retort formed in his eyes as he sat up in the bed. I didn't want to hear it, so I pounced. "Do you want to stay friends?" I asked, rushed and angry.

He nodded. "Of course."

"Do you want me to stay on as your secretary?"

He hesitated for a moment. Then he said, "I want what's best for you."

His answer, not what I expected, nearly brought me to my knees. But I used it to my advantage. "What is best for me is for you to continue with Jasmine. Marry her and pay me my fifteen grand. Understand?"

I knew I'd hurt him. I'd been cruel and callous. But I'd been even harder on myself. I'd opened us both up, laid us bare, then shut the door. It was ripping me apart.

Bobby slowly stood. He kissed my cheek and then moved around me, gathering up his clothes. He didn't say a word as he got dressed. He walked to the door of my shitty apartment and paused. He stood there, hand on the knob, forehead against the frame for what seemed like an eternity.

I warred with myself to stop him, to say something, anything. But I didn't. I stayed silent, and eventually, he left.

****

After one awkward day at the office, Hayden and I had managed to get our groove back. We worked together as if nothing had happened in our personal lives. And then on Thursday, the day before he left for his weekend with Jasmine, we regained our easy friendship as well.

Hayden took me out to lunch, and we gossiped about all of his execs and who was sleeping with whom. We compared notes on our knowledge about what Jack and Candace, Chelsea and Henry, and Grace and Meno were up to.

And I was hopeful, for the first time since the disastrous night I'd shown him the painting, that we could be friends again.

Friday, however, was painful. I went to work to hold down the fort while Hayden took his very first day off since taking over as CEO. I sat in his office, on his computer, answering his e-mails and taking his calls.

The chair held the faintest scent of him. A few of the pens were mangled with teeth marks where he'd chewed them with his talented mouth. The keys on his computer showed patterns of wear in the places his skilled fingers had touched them again and again.

Everything reminded me that I liked him touching me, kissing me, making love to me. And no amount of work or restored friendship was going to change that.

Late in the afternoon, I was perusing a document on the laptop when my cell phone rang. I smiled when a picture of Bobby, taken at the ballgame, came up on my screen. He looked so happy in that picture. He also looked smoking hot. He wore the Giants shirt I'd gotten him, and it clung to his thick muscles. His hair was mussed up from having been confined under a ball cap and then suddenly freed. And the genuine smile on his face made him look every bit as charming as he was.

"Why are you calling?" I asked in a teasing tone. "You should be banging right now." Even as I threw the line away casually, I flinched at the thought.

"She's gone."

"What?!"

"She left. I think I might need your help to sort things out. One of my cars is parked at the work garage, the red one, I think. Maybe you could…"

"Shit!" I didn't stop to think about what I should be

doing in this situation. I just did what I *wanted* to do. "I'll be right there."

Chapter 11

Hayden
One month ago

"Hey there, Chuck." I was pleased as hell to see her. But I didn't let on. I lounged on a beach towel, my head propped up on another rolled up towel, one of the white ones from the resort. Between my large aviator sunglasses and the careful set of my jaw, I was certain I looked casual and carefree.

"Son of a bitch," she grumbled as she slammed herself down on the sand beside me.

I tried not to smile when I saw the pissed-off look on her face. Instead, I went with innocent. "Sorry, it didn't work out."

"What the fuck, Bobby!"

"I didn't think you'd actually come out here." That was total bullshit. I'd hoped to hell she'd come all the way out there after I'd called and told her that Jasmine had taken off.

"Hayden. Robert. Morrison. What the fuck did you do?"

I almost drooled like an idiot. She was so hot when she was pissed at me. I turned away and looked up at the perfect blue sky to keep from giving myself away. "Why do you assume *I* did something?"

"Because I'm not stupid."

"How was the drive?" I asked her.

"Arrrggghh!" She pounded her fists into the beach, causing sand to fly up around us.

The bathers on the beach a few dozen yards away were undoubtedly staring at us, but I couldn't summon the will to care. I was too busy suppressing the massive grin on my face.

I gave her a few minutes, letting the quiet sit between us. In the background, I could hear the sound of young adults playing on the beach, screaming women, growling men. As an adults-only resort, play usually reserved for more private places tended to be permitted on the beach. That served me just fine, because Meg's presence and her anger were pitching a tent in my swim trunks.

Beneath the cacophony of the resort guests came the rough sound of the surf, the screeching cry of gulls, and closer to me, the comforting whisper of Meg taking deep breaths. When I turned to her, I half expected to see her in a yoga position. Instead, she leaned back on her elbows, her face pointed to the sky, her eyes closed.

I sat up and pulled off my sunglasses so I could get a better look. She wore a short, casual skirt, showing off her beautiful brown legs. She must have changed before heading up here because she wasn't in work clothes. Instead, my deepest wish had come true in the form of a tight tank top that curved around her full figure, showing the hint of a lacey bra beneath it. Her dark hair hung behind her head, pooling in the sand beneath her like an inky spill.

I could have watched her like that forever. Except that she opened her eyes and sat up abruptly, bringing her face within a couple feet of my own. I wasn't sure if she could see the desire in my eyes, but I didn't try to hide it.

We sat there for a long beat, just staring at each other. Then I leaned forward and kissed her. She didn't try to stop me. She didn't hang back, either. She threw her arms over my shoulders, put one hand in my hair, and pulled me closer.

My hands went to her waist, and I clung to her as she opened up to me, soft, rough, angry, and hungry. I thought I might die as I pushed her back into the sand, shifting so our bodies were aligned.

She moaned when my knee crept between her legs and moved up swiftly to rub against her in just the right spot.

"Bobby," she whispered, pulling away from me just enough to speak.

I tilted my head to attack her neck and asked quietly against her throat, "Yeah?"

"There are people."

I'd forgotten about them. And truthfully, I couldn't care less about them. I wanted to take her right there. But she sounded nervous, unhappy.

"I can't stop, baby," I said softly, kissing her neck.

She laughed. "I know. But I'm not into exhibition. I don't care what kind of resort this is." She pushed on my shoulders, and reluctantly I moved back so I could look at her. She smiled sweetly. "Take me to your room."

"With pleasure."

I scooped Meg up and threw her over my shoulder. Abandoning all of my gear, I made my way quickly up the hill toward the little bungalow I'd rented for the weekend. Meg didn't shriek like some women did when you carried them. Instead, her deep, throaty laugh chased us up to the room.

When we reached the door to the bungalow, I set her down and fumbled for the keycard tucked into the pocket of my trunks.

"Wait." Meg's hand landed on my upper arm as I moved the card toward the lock.

"What is it?" I asked, suddenly terrified of rejection.

"Did you have sex with Jasmine in there?" She nudged her head toward the door.

"No. I didn't have sex with Jasmine at all. I swear." I held my fingers in a scout's honor sign.

She looked at me for a long moment, her eyes narrowed.

"I didn't. I mean it. You can call her," I said, silently praying that she'd believe me. It *was* the truth, after all. I hadn't even been able to kiss Jasmine because all I wanted was Meg.

The expression on her face changed abruptly. "Open the door," she demanded.

I didn't hesitate. I shoved the keycard into the lock and swung the door open. Then I wrapped my arm around Meg's waist and swept her into the room before shutting the door behind us. I pulled Meg back to me and picked up where we left off on the beach.

It had been almost a week since we'd last made love, but it felt like an eternity and I was desperate for her. Meg's enthusiasm matched my own. She tugged on my swim trunks until they were a colorful puddle at my feet. I stepped out of them and backed her toward the bed.

"You are still wearing so many clothes," I

complained between kisses.

She chuckled in that low, raspy tone I loved. Then she pushed me away and stepped back until her legs hit the bed. She gave me a mischievous grin before ripping off her tank top and throwing it to the floor, followed by her skirt, which she slipped easily down her legs.

"Let me ask you a question, Bobby."

"Sure. Anything. Just keep stripping," I begged.

She put her hands behind her upper back but paused. "Do you like looking at me?"

She knew the answer to this question, of course. But I thought I understood why she asked. So I waited for a beat and was rewarded as she dropped the bra, exposing her perfect, ample breasts. "Hell, yes."

She poised her thumbs at the top of her panties. "You don't think I'm too…"

"Hot, sensuous, gorgeous, absolutely perfect?" I guessed.

Her smile grew wider. "I was going to say pudgy."

"What the fuck would give you that stupid idea?" I nodded my head at her, eyes on the red panties. "You gonna take those off?"

She laughed. But, disappointingly, she didn't finish the job. I took a step closer. She didn't stop me, but her gaze held a warning. She wasn't done yet.

"A few of my ex-boyfriends were fond of hinting I should spend more time at the gym."

"Fuck them." I took that last step toward her and pulled her to me by the waist. I nestled my head into her neck. "You are perfect. Absolutely perfect. I have never been so attracted to anyone in my life."

She yanked the panties off and kicked them away. My hands immediately found her amazing ass as I lowered her to the bed. I kissed and licked my way down her chest. "The question is, do you find me as attractive as I find you?" As soon as I asked the question, I pulled her left nipple into my mouth.

She moaned. When I released her nipple and kept working my way down, she took two hard breaths then answered me. "Are you kidding, Bobby?" She ran a hand over my upper back. "I painted you clothed. But when I do the naked version, it will be my masterpiece. And I could never do you justice."

I kissed my way to her bellybutton, then lower. "So you like me for my body?"

She sucked in air as I pulled her thighs apart and my breath hit her right where she wanted me most. "Hmmm. Yes. And your tongue."

I smiled to myself for a moment, then I used my tongue to make her scream.

****

"What happened with Jasmine?"

I leaned back in the booth, pushing my empty plate to the side and picking up my gin and tonic. "You've been dying to know, haven't you?"

We'd spent the rest of the afternoon in bed. Around eight, we took a shower and walked down to the resort's seaside restaurant for a late meal. We hadn't discussed my doomed date once all through dinner. Instead, I'd convinced Meg to tell me about her latest artwork pieces, her upcoming gallery show, and the studio she was hoping to get with my money.

But time was up, and now I had to spill.

To my surprise, Meg shrugged. "I kinda forgot about her." She looked guilty. "But now I want to know, yeah."

I chuckled. I liked the idea that she'd gotten caught up in me. I was always caught up in her these days. Of course, that was part of what went wrong with Jasmine. But I couldn't tell her that.

"It started to go bad on the drive here. I'm not a morning person."

I might get to work at insane hours these days, but only because I had trouble sleeping. I never really conjured up any joy about being awake until after Meg arrived at work and we drank our morning coffee together.

"I know," she said, grinning.

"I picked her up at her place, and I was still working on my coffee. So I didn't say much."

"In other words, you didn't say a damn thing for the whole ride, did you?"

I shrugged. "I said some things. Especially after she started harassing me."

"Harassing you?"

I sighed. This was where I had to admit my fault. Sure, I could've spun it to try to blame the whole thing on Jasmine. I might have even gotten away with it. I excelled at negotiation and spin. But they always seemed to fail me with Meg. I had a bad habit of always telling her the naked truth.

"She wanted to talk. So she started asking me a litany of questions."

Meg cocked her head to one side. It was freaking adorable. "What kind of questions?"

I took a sip of my drink and settled back in the seat before continuing with my confession. "They were normal questions. You know, about work, my family. But I didn't really…engage."

She folded her arms over her chest and gazed at me. She didn't look nearly as mad as I thought she would. "So you shut her out. What happened when you got here?"

I dipped my head for a moment. Then I looked back up at her. Her big, beautiful eyes met my own unflinchingly. One corner of her perfect, kissable mouth ticked up.

"More of the same," I admitted. "To be honest, by the time we got here, I was really cranky. And I was very tired of all the questions. I just couldn't manage to be Mr. Bright and Cheery."

Meg laughed, and I watched her, entranced. I remembered thinking, all through the drive here, that I'd wished it were Meg in the passenger seat beside me.

"So, she got pissed and left?"

"She got pissed, and I offered to pay for her to take a cab back."

"A cab?" She said, eyes wide. "That's going to cost a fortune! A ride share would have been much cheaper."

I chuckled. "Meg, I'm rich, remember?"

She smiled and looked down at the nearly empty plate in front of her, as if reminding herself she'd just eaten a meal that cost more than her entire outfit.

"I forget sometimes."

I leaned forward, reaching my body toward hers across the table. "I like it when you forget," I said in a low voice.

Her body leaned toward mine in turn, as if drawn to me. She licked her lips. "I seem to completely forget every time you take off your clothes." Her eyes dropped down to the *V* at the top of my button-up Hawaiian shirt.

"Let's go to my expensive bungalow and pretend I'm a homeless squatter."

****

I woke up to the sun streaming through the wispy window coverings in the one-room bungalow. By habit, I glanced at the bedside clock, which I could see over Meg's head. It read seven thirty. I hadn't slept this late in seven months.

I'd been suffering from pretty intense insomnia since taking the reins at Morrison and Sons. I tended to wake up in the middle of the night, work out, and go in to the office at the crack of dawn.

I looked down at the woman tangled in my arms and knew she was the reason I'd slept like a rock last night. Her silky hair, the color of the deep bark in a northern forest, spilled out on the pillow. Her face, relaxed and beautiful, snuggled against my chest. And her perfect body lay naked, her arms and legs intertwined with mine.

I'd nearly collapsed when she'd suggested she was anything but the most gorgeous specimen of a woman on the planet last night. I hated every man who'd put any doubt in her mind. To me she was perfect.

I'd dated women of all shapes and sizes, but I tended toward women with darker skin and ample curves. I wasn't into pale, thin girls, like my sister. Maybe it was why I'd instantly been attracted to Candace when I met her.

I considered Meg to be even hotter than Candace. While both women had incredible curves and creamy, dark skin, Candace stood nearly as tall as me. But Meg was short with tiny hands and feet. At first glance, it made it her look adorable. But then she opened her mouth and her feisty personality could easily belong to someone ten feet tall.

Everything about her intrigued me. I'd been happy when we became friends and thrilled when we started sleeping together. But then I saw that painting of me. It had been a shock for sure. I knew she was a talented artist. So the amazing likeness and the detail with which she'd created the rendering was not surprising.

But what did surprise the shit out of me was the discovery that Meg knew me better than anyone else on the planet. She'd painted it right there on the canvas, the conflict inside me, the contradiction of my life, the duality of my soul.

Jack, and to a certain extent Chelsea, knew me pretty well. They understood things about me that no one else did. But even they didn't see how my responsibility to my family and my need to stay true to myself had woven themselves into my life.

No one saw me like Meg did. And it made me want her even more.

I'd known at that moment I had to change the course of this dating thing. I hadn't wanted to go further with Jasmine anyway. Not because she wasn't a great girl. She was. Under other circumstances, I would have jumped at the chance to be with her. But I didn't want just a good woman anymore. I wanted Meg.

So, yeah, I'd sabotaged things with Jasmine. But even then, I wasn't sure Meg would have me again. She'd been clear the other night at her apartment about that. And I knew she couldn't accept me as something more, not when Hayden came as part of the package with "her Bobby."

So when Meg had shown up on the beach and fallen back into my bed, I felt like I'd won the lottery. Now I had to figure out how to keep her there.

Chapter 12

"I can't believe I wasted my entire weekend," Meg whispered, her lips brushing against a particularly sensitive spot on my torso.

Still breathing hard and reeling from the incredible oral sex she'd just given me, it took me a minute to be offended. "*Wasted?*"

She chuckled and kissed my bellybutton before moving up on the bed to lie beside me. I rolled over and propped my head up on my arm so I could look down at her.

"Seriously? Wasted?"

She reached up and stroked my scruffy chin with two fingers. "Don't get worked up, Bobby. I just meant that I had plans, things to get done. I didn't expect to spend the entire weekend here with you."

It was Sunday afternoon. Meg had spent two nights and the better part of three days with me at the resort. We'd hung out at the beach, gone whale watching, and I'd attempted to teach her to surf. We'd also eaten our fill, sipped on fantastic wine, and made love over and over again.

"It's been the best weekend I've had in…a really fucking long time," I blurted out, still offended.

"Hey…" She reached up and kissed me softly. "I had fun, too. I'm glad your date went south and I got to spend this time with you."

This placated me, and I relaxed a little. She ran her finger from my chin down to my chest, and it left a delicious trail of fire in its wake.

"I was just thinking about what excuse I'm going to make."

"Excuse?" I'd gone on to thinking about what I wanted to do to her naked body, so I wasn't tracking.

"Yeah, I was supposed to have lunch with Candace and Chelsea yesterday. Grace is coming home next month, and we wanted to plan a party. I rescheduled by text, just saying I'd gone out of town. But when I meet up with them tomorrow, they're going to ask me where I've been. And I'll sit there, looking like I got laid for three straight days and afraid to lie to my best friend and your sister."

Grace was a fascinating subject, and it almost distracted me. The latest word was that she planned to come back to SF to deal with the house she'd gotten in the divorce. No one knew if Meno intended to come back with her or not.

But I wasn't deterred. "Why do you have to lie?"

She gave me a look of exasperation. "I can't tell the truth."

Perhaps ego had reared its ugly head, or maybe even some form of jealousy. Regardless, her need for secrecy bothered me. Every middle-child insecurity I'd suffered in my life came to the surface when she said things like that. I knew I'd agreed to keep us a secret, but that was before the painting, before our weekend, before I realized I didn't want anyone else, maybe ever.

"Why not?" I asked.

Meg eased the sting by running her hand from my chest to my abs, where it flattened out and made a burning path straight down. Instantly hard again in her firm grip, I pouted.

"I just don't think it's a good idea," she said, her voice filled with reason. "But you know what I *do* think is a good idea."

I was on fire, but I restrained myself, waiting. "What?" I practically croaked.

"Having a little more fun before we drive back."

Without further discussion, I rolled on top of her and turned her idea into reality.

****

Three weeks ago

I leaned back on my heels and gazed up at her. She perched on the edge of my desk. Her head thrown back in ecstasy; her elbows propped up her torso across a stack of folders. Her wide princess skirt pooled up on the desk, one side of it resting on my laptop, the other over the phone. I had no idea what I'd done with her panties in my haste to get my mouth on her. Now she was deeply satisfied, and I could watch her, take her in.

"Jesus, Bobby," she mumbled lazily.

We stayed like that for a long, luscious moment. Then her eyes snapped open, and she sat forward. Something rich and feral shone in them as she reached for me. She grabbed a handful of my hair and tugged.

I obeyed her command. I had no choice. She was an addiction for me, one that controlled my every thought and desire. Once I was standing in front of her, she unbuckled my belt and lithely undid the button and zipper of my pants, her fingers fast and nimble.

"You're amazing, Chuck," I told her.

She raked my pants down to my knees, and gripping my ass, she pulled me to her roughly. She was ready for me, and I slid into her in one easy, intense movement.

I grunted. She cried out. I put my hand over her mouth and said on a chuckle, "Pretty sure the office walls aren't very thick, baby." I took my hand away to kiss her.

She accepted my kiss, but then pulled back. "And I didn't lock the door," she said, a challenging smile on her lips. Then she lay back on the desk and planted her heels into the back of my thighs. "Better make it quick, before someone comes to investigate," she said breathlessly.

I gave her exactly what she wanted, and what I desperately needed. I slid into her again and again until we came together, her with a silent scream, me with a repressed groan.

For a long time after, I lay with my head resting on her stomach, both of us just breathing. Eventually, she shifted, and I let her up. We stood in front of my desk. I pulled up my pants while she tried to locate her underwear.

"Seriously, what did you do with them?" she asked, throwing her hands up in the air.

I put my arm around her waist and tugged her toward me. "No idea. Hey, that was a great meeting, by the way."

We were supposed to be discussing a request for proposal that Candace wanted to put out for bid on some historic restoration work. I had been having trouble pulling up the file, and she'd come around the desk to help me. The next thing I knew, she was on the desk with me on my knees worshiping her.

Meg looked up at me, stroking my face with her

hand. "That was sooo bad." She grinned, and I knew that she cared about propriety about as much as I did.

"I didn't use a condom," I said, the guilt painted on my face.

"Hmmmm. Well, are you clean?"

I nodded. "Yeah, I've been tested, but—"

"Me too. Just last month."

"Yeah, but what about—" I began.

"I have an IUD," she said, interrupting my concern about birth control before I could voice it.

"Really?"

"Yeah," She bit her lip. "The boyfriend before last…he, um…he used to trick me. He'd take the condom off halfway through sex."

"What the fuck!" I said, incensed.

"I dumped him after he did it twice. But I learned my lesson. I wasn't going to take my chances."

"Meg…" I wanted to tell her she was so much better than the dickheads she'd dated. I wanted to tell her I'd kick all their asses for her because of how she'd been treated. But nothing came out, and she took the opportunity to change the conversation.

"What I meant was, we didn't lock the door. We'll have to remember to do that next time. I think we're damn lucky we didn't get walked in on." She gestured to the door with her head.

"Yeah, Candace is due up here in a few minutes, and she has been known to be early," I agreed.

A strange look crossed her face. "She'd knock. But your dad…"

"He wouldn't knock. But he's on a golf course in Sausalito right now, I think we're safe. Jack, on the other hand. If he decided to stop by, or Chelsea, neither of them would knock. And if they heard us, they'd be even more likely to barge in and find out what's going on." I grinned.

"Hmmm. It's too bad I didn't get a chance to see my favorite part of you."

I cocked my head at her. "It's not—"

"Okay, let me rephrase," she said, pulling my shirt out of my pants and unbuttoning it from the bottom up. "My favorite part to stare at while I'm playing with my other favorite part." She pulled my shirt open, exposing my chest and abs. Then she ran her hands slowly from my neck to my hips. "Damn, Bobby. You are like a sculpture." She ran a finger through a groove in my muscles. "Peaks and valleys, immaculately formed."

"So I guess I should be glad I spent all those years bodybuilding."

"God, yes." She kept up the ministrations with her hands but ripped her gaze away from my body to look up into my face. "Is that why you started bodybuilding? To get girls?"

I shrugged. "I don't know exactly why I started. I was restless in my youth. I picked this to do, and it stuck. It was mostly the action of working out that I liked. But I admit that competing in college helped my self-esteem, too, at a time when I really needed it."

"Do you still compete?"

I chuckled. "No. And I'm too busy to stay in that kind of shape anyway. I just work out now as habit, I guess. I still like it. But I do less weight training and more cardio these days." She looked at me like I said something important, even though it was just babble about my workouts. "Why are we talking about this? It's not something that interests you," I said, taking a step back.

She laughed. "You're right, I only run when I'm being chased. But that doesn't mean what you do isn't interesting to me. And, I have to admit, I certainly wouldn't mind watching you work out. That would be very entertaining to me."

I buttoned up my shirt while she watched. "We could maybe do that sometime." The only women who'd ever seen me work out were the ones that did it with me. But the idea of Meg sitting in a corner of my home gym watching me made me hard all over again.

I tucked my shirt into my pants. "Candace really will be here soon. We should find your panties."

I started the search again, but Meg didn't move. "You have a thing for her, don't you?"

I was looking beneath the desk when she said it, and I hit my head coming up. "What?"

"Candace. You have a thing for her." It was a statement, not a question. And it pissed me off.

"No."

"No?"

We stood, facing each other, arms at our sides, lips pressed together.

"Why would you even say that?" I asked.

"You forget we didn't just meet last month, Bobby. From the first time I met you, I saw how you looked at her. I saw the petulant set of your jaw every time Jack touched her. You wanted her. Don't deny it."

"I *did*. But that was a long time ago."

"And…it's gone away?"

I was still angry. "Yes. It's gone away. What do you think? I am still pining after my brother's wife? What kind of asshole do you think I am?"

"I don't think you're an asshole at all."

I knew this, but it still struck me how things had changed between us. Two months ago, she would have elaborated on exactly what kind of asshole I was. And I stood there for a moment, silently staring at her.

Meg moved away from our showdown, backing away from the desk, toward the door. "I'm going to get some work done. I need to send that memo for you, and I have to find you your next date."

It was the first time she'd said anything about a date for me since Jasmine. I'd started to think maybe she would drop the whole thing. I didn't like her finding me a date. And I didn't like her walking away from me. In fact, I hated it.

"Why don't *you* go out with me?"

This stopped her backward motion. Her feet froze, one behind the other. "What?"

I took a step toward her. "Yeah, we could go to a show, or just dinner. Whatever you want."

Even though we'd technically gone out a bunch of times, to ball games, to lunch, to dinner, for drinks, and hell, even an entire weekend at a beach resort, this was the first time I'd actually asked her on a date. The significance was not lost on her.

"No." Her answer, spoken so softly I almost didn't hear it, was firm and decided.

Before I could ask her why, she ducked out the door.

****

Two weeks ago

"I don't understand. Sandy's not even a year old yet, but she's enrolled in some kid-genius thing?" I knew I sounded critical, but I had been sure my brother would raise his daughter very differently from how we were raised. And now, as we strolled around Lake Merritt on a bright, sunny day, he was telling me about some weird program my niece had just started.

Jack laughed. "No. It's not a genius thing, dumbass. It's a playgroup. You know, a way to socialize. She'll eat mud pies with other kids, that kind of thing. We started the program for poor kids in the Tenderloin who are in isolated situations. And now we're taking Sandy. She's an only child, there aren't any other kids in our building, and she doesn't have any cousins yet." He smirked. "So, it's a fun thing we think will be good for her."

I nodded. "We kinda grew up in an isolated situation, didn't we?"

Jack and I never talked about our childhood. I peeked at him out of the corner of my eye. He walked slowly beside me on the path, his head down. But I could see he'd turned somber with this subject, thoughtful. Maybe Jack was as desperate to break the wall between us as I was.

We'd been getting along a lot better since that fateful day many years ago when I tried to sabotage his relationship with Candace. But we were still not where we'd been when we were little kids. Before high school, Jack had been my best friend. He was all I had. I had wrecked that, and I had no idea how to put it back together again. But somehow, I felt like if I quit overanalyzing it and went with the tides, things would work between us.

"We did," Jack finally said. "We didn't even play with other kids. It wasn't until we were sent to boarding school that we really had other people to interact with.

And then we made friends, and they were ripped away from us all summer. Then we'd get switched to another school. It's not what I want for Sandy. I want her to have what Candie had growing up."

"Hippy kidfest," I teased.

"Yeah, sounds great, doesn't it?"

I nodded. "Yeah, it does." I tasted the words I was about to say in my mouth before letting them go. "When you were Sandy's age, you were all alone. I was lucky. I had you from the very beginning."

Jack didn't respond to this. But I could see the small smile on his lips. After all these years, I'd said something genuinely kind and meaningful to him. I could see that he was pleased.

But he knew better than to make a big deal out of it, and I was grateful when he changed the subject. "Tell me how the hunt for a wife is going."

"Does everyone know about that?"

"Of course. First of all, Henry told us all over the brunch you missed the morning after the wedding. And, of course, Meg told Candie. Everyone knows."

I shrugged. "I kinda figured. Mom was super weird last time I went to the house."

"She's stoked. She can't wait for you to bring home some hand-picked princess to be your rock while you carry on the family legacy."

I winced a little. Jack was trying to be light. He didn't know how much I felt the weight of that legacy on my shoulders. I looked away, admiring the way the sun reflected on the water.

Jack's hand landed on my shoulder. "Truth is, Hayden, you are the perfect person to represent us all. To carry on what Grandpa and Dad started. To make it better. You always were."

I stopped walking and moved to a bench at the side of the path. Jack followed me. We sat side by side for a moment in silence while I absorbed what he'd said. Jack wouldn't lie. He wouldn't blow smoke. Which meant he really believed that.

I leaned back in my seat. "I need some advice, big brother."

"From me? I don't know shit about business, Hayden. I'm a college dropout who runs a nonprofit. And believe me, there is *no* profit."

"I don't mean that. I mean about women." I turned to look at him, a smirk on my face. "I know you know a lot about that."

Jack had been a major player before he'd settled down with Candace. He'd always been much better at that than me. I'd tried to live up to my big brother's Casanova reputation and failed.

"Okay. What's up?"

"So, there's one woman I'm really interested in."

"Is she one of the girls Meg set you up with?"

"No," I answered quickly. "She's outside of all that. But, um, she won't go out with me."

"Shot you down, huh?"

"Yeah."

"So. Move on."

"I don't want to. I want *this* woman."

Jack studied my face, his own expression unreadable. "What kind of interactions have you had with her up to this point? I mean, have you known her for a while? Did you just meet? Are you friends?"

"I've known her for a while, and we're..." I hesitated. Too much information would lead Jack to the truth. But I also needed to lay it out there for him. At the same time, I didn't really know how to define Meg and me. "We're friends. And, um, we've been sleeping together for a few weeks."

Jack's eyebrows raised. "Wait. You've been sleeping with this woman. This is going on while Meg is setting you up on dates? And this woman, even though she's sleeping with you, she won't go out with you?"

"That about sums it up, yeah. But for the record, I haven't slept with any of the women Meg set me up with."

"Is this woman sleeping with anyone other than you?"

My chest ached with the thought. "I don't think so."

"Okay…So you are basically in a monogamous relationship with someone who doesn't want to date you, while at the same time going out on numerous dates with women you don't want."

I knew I looked guilty, but I couldn't help it. I *was* guilty. "Yep."

Jack blew out a long breath. "Damn, little brother. How the hell did you end up in this situation?"

"Believe me, Jack. I've been asking myself the same thing."

"Do you love her?"

The question was like a bucket of cold water. It stung my flesh and chilled me to the bone. In a split second, I knew the answer. Knew it, but couldn't say it.

Chapter 13

"Hayden?" Jack watched me, waiting.

I said nothing.

"So…I'm going to take that as a yes. You *do* love this mystery woman."

I didn't acknowledge it verbally, and I didn't nod. I just looked into Jack's eyes.

He smiled. "You don't have to look so glum about it. I know it's hard to swallow. But I promise, in the end, it's a good thing."

"Says the man who convinced his girl to marry him. I can't even get mine to go out on a date with me."

"I had a hard time at first, too," he said. "You should trick her into a date."

"What?" I looked at him like he'd grown a second head.

"Yeah. You hang out as friends all the time, right?"

"Right."

"So, go somewhere and then turn it into a real date. The key is, you have to, at some point, tell her you are having a date so it's different from every other time you go out."

"That's when she'll get pissed at me," I predicted.

He shrugged. "You gotta confront it, man. You gotta *make* her acknowledge your relationship."

I nodded.

"I can't wait to meet this one," he said, amusement

in his voice.

"Hey, I heard Grace is coming back to town in a couple weeks. What do you know about that?" I asked, purposely changing the subject.

"What I know is"—he leaned forward, conspiratorially—"the last time I talked to Meno, I could tell something was up. It was in his voice. I think they're sleeping together."

"What does Candace think?"

"When I asked her, she started by telling me what Grace *says*. She's working at the restaurant, and that's good for her wounded soul right now. That she needs to learn to work because she signed a prenup and isn't getting much out of the divorce. That Meno is just a friend helping her out. But when I pressed her, she admitted she thinks they're sleeping together, too."

My palms were a little sweaty, and I rubbed them on my jeans. I wondered if this secret Meg was so determined to keep from my family wasn't already being bandied about in Candace and Jack's living room.

****

What I had done was a little deceitful. Meg wanted to talk about some dating prospects Monday after work. But of course, she didn't want to go out to dinner with me because that would be too much like a date. Now that she was on alert for that, she'd been more and more difficult about even having lunch alone with me at a restaurant on workdays.

So I told her I hadn't had a chance to work out that morning and I wanted to go home to do that, then, afterward, I'd make us both dinner.

I left it up to Meg whether or not she wanted to join me just for dinner or if she wanted to talk while I went through my workout routine. I knew which one she would pick.

"So, um, you don't do the treadmill for longer than that?" she asked, eyeing my bare chest lasciviously.

"No, I used it for an hour this morning, so I'm just doing twenty minutes to warm up and then hitting the weights." I moved onto the bench and lay down beneath the weights I'd already set.

She looked around the room filled with equipment. "I can't believe I didn't know this was even here."

"I keep the door closed. It has a separate ventilation system."

"It's so big for a spare bedroom," she observed.

"It's actually a second master," I explained, gesturing to the bathroom that sat off the room. "I had the carpet replaced with mat, moved my equipment in, and voilà."

"Some people have home offices. You have a home gym." She did not sound critical as she said it.

"And you have a studio in your living room."

"Touché."

I concentrated on doing reps. I wanted to turn Meg on, but getting hurt wouldn't quite do it. When I finished the bench press, I looked over at her. Her eyes were bright and wide, her cheeks and neck flushed.

I moved to the shoulder machine. "You said you wanted to watch me work out. What do you think?"

She was perched on a rolling stool, her back resting against the side bar of the treadmill. Her hands were twisted together in her lap. "I should be videotaping this. I could go to freaking Beverly Hills and show it around, and I would have a flock of high-class women knocking down your door."

I stood and took the two short steps over to her. I leaned down and kissed her gently on the mouth. "I don't really care what other women think," I said truthfully. "I care what *you* think."

She ran her hand up my torso. "I like. Do more."

I chuckled and walked back to the machine to start my reps. Eventually, Meg remembered her task and started talking about dates for me while I worked my way around the equipment.

"Okay, first up is Kimberley Wains. She's twenty-eight, works as a financial planner, and went to USF. I met her at a fundraiser Candace's mom put together about two years ago. We kept in touch via Facebook. Anyway, she's kind, smart, and single. And gorgeous. She's one of those tall blondes with legs that go on forever. Want to see a picture?"

I shook my head. I wasn't going to find any woman as a hot as the one in front of me now. What was the point?

"Second—and these are in order from least likely to most likely, by the way—is Jennifer Graham. She's thirty-one. She's a junior editor at a publishing company with a bright future there. She's super smart and, obviously, a bookworm. But she's fun, too. She definitely knows how to let her hair down. She's really pretty, especially her face. But, like me, she's more filled out."

"Curvy?" I suggested.

"Yes. And short. Some people would call it pudgy."

"I would call it hot as hell," I reminded her.

She blushed. "I think she's a good prospect."

"Where did you meet her?" I asked.

"She's in my book club."

I mulled that over. "Book club, huh? That seems very normal and tame for you, Chuck. Domestic even."

"Whatever. I refuse to address that," she said hotly. "Let's move on to number three, shall we? This is the one I think will interest you the most. Her name is Heather Yarborough. She's a fellow artist. She rents a studio in the same building I used to have one in. She does sculpture, and she's very talented."

I stopped doing leg lifts and sat up on the bench so I could look her in the eye. "You're setting me up with an artist?"

She nodded. "You appreciate creativity, and artists are a little more carefree. That will be good for you."

Frustration rose. I ran a hand through my hair. "But I thought…" What did I say? I thought you didn't want to officially be with me because a CEO and an artist didn't fit together? I could say that, but then she might tell me the real reason she didn't want to be with me. And I wasn't sure I could handle that.

"Heather comes from a wealthy family," she explained. "She grew up a lot like you. Went to boarding school, all that. And like you, she rebelled. She had a wild youth. But now she's ready to settle down. She's always getting offers from guys all over the studio because she's gorgeous, like model gorgeous. But she's particular. And *she* was the one who asked *me* about *you*."

Despite the talk about another woman, Meg was still turned on by what was happening in front of her. As her eyes roamed my body, her cheeks turned pink. Somehow she'd been able to stay focused on this asinine conversation about dates while still watching me and succumbing to the feelings that invoked.

I wanted to distract her. But Meg was a multitasker by nature, and that wasn't easy to do. So I flexed my muscles, clenching down on the bench so my biceps popped out. Her eyes showed me what it did to her.

"Come here," I said quietly.

She stood and moved fluidly to me. Like always, she wore a skirt. And without me asking, she pulled her skirt to her waist and sat on my thighs.

"So, which one do you want to date?" she asked, looping her arms around my shoulders.

"None," I whispered. Then I leaned in and kissed her. When she was full on melting, I pulled back. "I want to date *you*." I felt her stiffen and she tried to get up, but I held her on my lap. "Don't run away. I know the answer is no. I'm just being honest." I reached my hand down between her legs and rubbed gently.

Her head fell back. "I can't date you, Bobby."

I kissed her neck. "Okay. But will you stay the night?" I asked, increasing the pressure with my fingers.

"God," she breathed. "I don't think I could make myself leave."

****

Since that night in my home gym, I'd managed to dodge Meg's attempts to set me up and kept her so preoccupied with sex, she hadn't pushed the issue. But I knew I couldn't hold her off forever. So, a week later, I took my brother's advice. Rather than continue to ask Meg out and get rejected again and again. I decided to take her out on a date without her knowing it.

When Jack had first proposed it on that bench by the lake, I'd had no idea how the hell I would pull it off.

But then the perfect opportunity had presented itself.

"Chuck," I said, throwing my office door open and stepping in front of her desk.

"Jesus, Hayden," she whispered, looking around frantically. "Don't call me that in public."

Her desk wasn't really in public. It sat in a vestibule off the main executive hallway. But as I turned around I realized what had upset her. A handful of people stood in the hallway. A few heads turned, one of which was the director of acquisitions and another was his assistant. They were talking to the marketing director and public relations coordinator. Caught staring, they all turned and bustled away.

I looked back at Meg and raised an eyebrow. "You don't like Chuck?"

She shook her head and sighed. "It's a little freaking *intimate*."

I really liked that. She thought our nicknames were intimate. "Is that why you call me Hayden at work?"

She bit her lip. "I think it's best we stay professional, yes."

I grinned at her. She had no idea how much I liked making her squirm. "Is that what we were doing in my office yesterday? Acting professional?"

She leaned forward. "You know what? If you want to ever do that again, you will drop this," she said angrily.

I suppressed my laughter, afraid I'd piss her off more.

"What do you need, *Hayden*?"

"I need you to gather up your stuff. We're going somewhere."

She looked at her watch. "Where are we going at

four thirty on a Friday?"

"What difference does it make what time it is?"

Meg stood up from her chair, pushing it into the wall behind her. She reached into the middle drawer of her desk and wrenched her purse out. "Fine. I'll go to a stupid meeting with you. But I am charging double time for this."

My smile grew impossibly larger. "Fine. Be sure to clock exactly how long it takes from now until you get back to your apartment tonight. I'll pay you triple for it."

Her eyes got wide, and finally she smiled. "See, now you're thinking with a straight head."

She walked around the desk and held out her arm. "Lead the way, boss."

Meg didn't argue as I ushered her to my car. And she quit asking where we were going after I refused to answer the first three times. Instead, she sat in the passenger seat playing with the radio and giving me a hard time. Just like always.

When we reached the old building on the pier, her interest peaked. "What are we doing here?"

"You ever been here before?" I asked as I slid the car into a spot.

"Sure. They do fashion shows down here sometimes, charity events, that kind of thing. Are we going to a charity event?"

"Not today." I opened my door and crawled out of the car.

I hurried to the other side, but I didn't get there in time to get Meg's door. She slipped out of the car and stared up at the building. People were trickling in, mostly dressed like us, for work. Some were coming from the tech industry side of town and were in jeans and hoodies. And a few older ladies had sailed over from the North Bay, dressed very much like my mother might be on a Friday afternoon.

"Bobby? What's up?" She looked at me with those perfect eyes, and I almost gave it away.

"Come see." I took her hand. She paused, looking at our hands linked together. "Don't worry," I reassured her. "No one from work or anyone in my family will be here. I'd know if they were planning to come."

This seemed to placate her, and she left her hand in mine, walking beside me into the building. Once we got inside, I enjoyed watching Meg's face as she took it all in. The pop-up art show was all the article I'd read promised it would be. It featured a combination of massive abstract sculptures, wall-sized paintings, and even bare concrete marked with spray paint.

"Big Beautiful Art," Meg breathed, looking up at the long vinyl banner that hung in the center of the massive open room.

We walked slowly through the exhibits, hand in hand. We talked a little, murmuring to one another about the pieces with "I really like that one" or "That's a little much" or "I need that over my couch."

I lost track of the time, but we were in there for over an hour. When we emerged onto the pier, I pulled Meg over to a bench overlooking the Bay. We both stared out at the water.

"I'm a little surprised you didn't know about this show," I told her.

"I've been busy as hell lately," she reminded me. "Working for you, setting you up on dates." She turned to look at me. "Sleeping with you." She gave me a blinding smile. "Thank you, Bobby. Thank you so much."

I shrugged. "It wasn't much."

She shook her head. "No. It was. I needed to slow down and look around me, and you made me do that today."

"Wanna keep doing it?"

She cocked her head. "What do you mean?"

I gestured with my head to the Bay. "Let's take a boat to Angel Island, walk around a little, and then have dinner at that grill there."

She gaped at me.

"Too slow?"

"Um…no. It sounds perfect, actually. I was just thinking we've probably already missed the last boat out there."

I plucked my phone out of my pocket. "Don't worry, I know a guy."

****

I reached over with my napkin and brushed the chocolate off her face.

She smiled at me and laughed. "God. I ate so fast. What a pig."

I shook my head. "Everything you do is graceful and perfect. Besides, you were hungry."

We'd strolled around the island until the sun began to set before settling in for a decadent meal out on the porch of the grill. As we finished up dessert, we looked out over the Bay. Despite the stunning view on the water, I couldn't take my eyes off Meg.

She pierced me with her glare and folded her arms across her chest. "Well, you did it, Bobby."

"Did what?"

"You tricked me into going out on a date with you."

Here I'd been trying to decide exactly how to out our date as Jack had suggested, and she'd already figured it out. I gaped at her in faux shock. "What? I have no idea what you're talking about," I said, in an exaggerated tone.

"Whatever. You asked me out on a date, and I said no. Which was stupid, because really, we go on dates all the time. So, to prove a point, you tricked me into this little rendezvous." She pursed her lips and stared at me, like she'd just proved the biggest point of her life.

"And?" I asked.

She pretended to be pissed for another minute, then her face fell and she chuckled. She leaned forward and kissed me quickly. "It worked. Point proven. I like going out with you, Bobby." Her face was close to mine, her breath hot against my lips. She spoke in a soft, seductive whisper. "I like spending time with you. I like kissing you." To demonstrate, she gave me another soft kiss. "And I will go home with you tonight. And tomorrow, you are going to take me to breakfast, then we are going to go my place and I am going to paint you, nude."

"And maybe, on Sunday, you could come with me to my family brunch?" I asked, knowing I was pushing the envelope.

Her face scrunched up. "I'll think about it while you're meeting my every need between now and then."

"Your wish is my command," I said. And I meant it.

Chapter 14

Meg
One week ago

"How exactly did you get roped into this again?" my best friend asked, a mischievous grin on her face.

I rolled my eyes. "I told you. It's business."

She looked at me as though she'd believe I could get her oceanside property in Arizona before she'd believe that.

"Meg and I are going outside for a minute," she announced to the entire Morrison clan, who were gathering at one end of the massive living room.

She tugged my arm, pulling me across the room, toward the sliding glass door, and out into the pool area of the Morrison mansion.

"We are alone," Candace said, stating the obvious. "You've been avoiding being alone with me for weeks. You've been acting weird. And now, you show up at the Morrison family Sunday brunch. What gives?"

"Have you ever seen that man beg?" I asked, pointing my thumb over my shoulder toward the house. "It's pathetic. I mean, really pathetic. He asked me to come. I agreed. That's all there is to it."

"He asked you to come because you're his secretary? Really?"

I tapped my foot on the ground. "What exactly are

you getting at?"

"He brought you here to meet his parents," she accused.

"Except I've already met them. First at your wedding, then at Chelsea's. And I've seen them both when they stop by the office."

"Are you sleeping with Hayden?"

Damn.

"What would make you say a thing like that?" I asked, trying to keep the panic from bubbling up in my throat and seeping into my words.

Candace narrowed her eyes and leaned toward me. "You are."

I should have known this would happen. I'd been caught in a weak moment when I'd agreed to come, a very weak moment. Not only had Hayden promised to take me to meet his former nanny, Sonya, after brunch if I went with him, he also happened to be doing very wicked things to me with his hands at the time.

"I am trying to find him a wife. Did it ever occur to you that one of the best ways to do that is to get to know his family better? I mean, I am a professional here. I have to cover all my bases."

"That is such a load of bull. You're sleeping with him."

I threw my head back and made a sound of exasperation. What I was really doing was avoiding her gaze.

"His mom loves you, you know," she said.

"Of course she does. I am finding her son a wife."

Candace shook her head. "No. I think it's more than that."

"We should go back in. They're going to wonder

what's going on," I complained.

"Fine," she said, huffy. She reached toward the door handle. "But just for the record. I think you're sleeping with Hayden."

"Think what you want, weirdo." I stepped past her into the house.

Seeing the home that Hayden, Jack, and Chelsea had grown up in had been a source of anxiety for me from the moment I'd agreed to come to the weekly family brunch. I had been in rich people's homes before. I'd been in my high school boyfriend's house a bunch of times, of course, and I'd done a few commissioned art pieces that required a home visit. I'd long lived under the assumption that rich people lived in fancy, sterile boxes that were wasteful in both space and opulence. I could never imagine one being something I could call a home—until I went to the Morrison's house.

Large, for San Francisco anyway, and regal, it was certainly well situated with an incredible view of the Bay. But it was also warm, the furniture functional and comfortable. The house was laid out to accommodate the flow of the people who lived there, rather than guests and dinner parties.

I knew plenty of fancy dinner parties had been held in this house. I knew hired helpers cleaned it and cooked in it. I even knew Jack and Hayden had considered it to be a bit of a gilded cage growing up. Still, there was something about it that soothed my nerves.

Maybe it wasn't the house at all. Maybe it was the people.

Despite her groomed-to-perfection appearance,

Frances Morrison exuded warmth and welcome to Candace and me. And she doted on all three of her kids. The affection was equal but manifested in different ways. She made sure Jack knew she heard him, Chelsea knew she saw her, and Hayden knew she appreciated him.

Hayden's dad, John, was a fascinating subject. Even before I'd met the man, Candace and I'd had conversations about him. On the surface, he seemed to be a hard-nosed businessman, cold and distant to everyone he spoke with. Yet, every word he said was measured, each sentiment crafted in honesty. And if a person listened closely, it became apparent that nothing—not business, money, or prestige—meant more to him than the happiness and well-being of his family. And he was ridiculously cute with his grandbaby.

"I'm glad you finally found a good assistant," John said to Hayden. "She will make your life so much better, believe me." His eyes sparkled as he turned my way.

Hayden turned to look at me for a brief moment before responding. "She's not just good. She's the best. But I'm afraid she's not going to be staying for long."

"Oh, no?" John said, his eyebrows raising.

I felt like I'd been transported back in the dining room of my high school boyfriend's house, his rich parents quizzing me, judging me. So I went on lockdown and stayed quiet.

When I didn't speak, Candace jumped in. "Meg has another career. She's just helping Hayden out during the transition."

This was it, the moment that my career became the

butt of all the jokes. I held my breath.

"Meg is an artist. A very accomplished artist," Hayden said. There was no mistaking the pride in his tone. "You know that piece in my bedroom?"

"The Presidio piece?" Frances asked.

"Yes. She did it."

"Oh, Meg. I just love that painting! I didn't realize that was yours. I told Hayden I wanted something by the same artist for my next birthday," Frances said.

I could feel my cheeks burning.

"I haven't forgotten, Mom. I just didn't get around to mentioning it to Meg yet. I still have three months." He grinned at me.

I had been to a few gallery shows where people gushed over my work. It was always a little embarrassing. But this…this was completely different.

"That painting," John said, pointing his fork at me, his look grave, "is incredible. If you have more like that, I don't know why you are wasting your time helping Hayden out."

"Dad!" Hayden exclaimed playfully.

"Don't talk her into leaving him, Dad," Jack said, laughing.

John blinked. "Sorry. It's my business brain. I just saw dollar signs. If you ever want some advice on selling your work, marketing, that kind of thing, you come to me, Meg. You have a great little business there. You'll do well."

Tears threatened to burn my eyes, and I had to excuse myself to go to the bathroom. It wasn't just the praise or the sincerity with which it was delivered. It was that, for the first time in my life, I felt like someone outside the art world believed in me.

****

Sonya might have been a tiny woman, but she was strong as hell. And that wasn't just meant figuratively. Within moments of our arrival, she'd challenged me to an arm-wrestling match. She'd won, and I hadn't given it to her either.

Moments after that, she'd made Bobby turn around in a circle in the center of the room so she could get a good look at him, remarking that the older he got, the cuter his butt got. He called her a dirty old lady and tried to convince her to let me find her a boyfriend so she could get laid and stop hitting on hot, young studs.

I laughed my ass off the whole time.

"I hate to say this, Hoss," she said, using her nickname for him. I thought it was perfect for Hayden who was, in so many ways, a gentle giant. "But I think she might be good enough for you." She pointed at me while looking at him.

"Are you kidding? Get your eyes checked, old lady. She's way out of my league."

Sonya shook her head slowly, taking me in with her shrewd eyes. "She's a little weak in the upper arms, but she's pretty and intelligent. And I can tell already that she doesn't put up with your bullshit."

"All true," he said, smiling.

"We're not actually…together," I said, feeling a need to put the brakes on this conversation right away.

Sonya laughed. "Whatever, sweetheart."

I stared at her, then I turned to Bobby. He shrugged but could not wipe the goofy grin off his face.

"You better tell her to do you better than that, Hoss," she told him.

He threw his hands up in the air. "I couldn't boss

around a classy lady like her. Hell, I'd have better luck bossing *you* around."

"In your dreams," she said. Then she turned to me, leaning in, her brown eyes narrowing. "Now listen here, missy. This one…" She put her hand on Bobby's knee. "He's special. Of all the kids I raised, ten of 'em for other people, plus four of my own, he's *the one*. If he'd been my peer instead of my kid, I'd a married him in a heartbeat."

My heart raced as I watched her, and I believed every word.

"Okay, quit harassing my girlfriend, old lady, or I won't bring her back. Let's get down to business."

My heart stuttered when Bobby called me his girlfriend, but I didn't say anything. Sonya and Bobby treated it as if it were completely normal.

Using her cane, Sonya lifted herself up out of the padded chair that sat beside Bobby and across from me at the small round table to one side of her spacious room. She shuffled over to the dresser.

Bobby watched her closely. "How's that hip?"

"Doc says it'll be just fine as long as I don't fall on it again."

She retrieved a stack of papers and brought them over to Bobby. She dropped them roughly on the table and sat back down. Her shrewd eyes turned on me. "Kid thinks he knows more than the doctors."

Bobby started leafing through the papers. "No, old lady, I just know that you are too stubborn to follow doctor's orders. I pay too much money for you to see a specialist and have you ignore what she tells you."

Nothing surprised me about the fact that Bobby paid her bills. And I knew, instinctively, that he wasn't complaining about the cost for any reason other than to get her to do what was best for her.

She waved her hand at him dismissively. But there was a definite sparkle in her eye when she turned back to me. "I've got all these kids, but none of them babies me the way Hoss does."

As I sat there and watched Bobby quiz Sonya about her medications and activity restrictions, a vision filled my head. If I was really this man's girlfriend, we'd come here together once a week and spend the afternoon with this incredible woman. Then we'd go home and he'd do with me what he does with her, take care of me. Because that's what Bobby did. He always thought about my comfort, my safety, and my money situation. He always worried about me eating enough or often enough, and he always wanted me to be happy.

No one had ever taken care of me growing up, and as an adult, when someone like Candace tried, I hated it, rejected it, threw it off like a suffocating blanket. But now I was letting Bobby do it in subtle ways every day, and I found that, much to my surprise, I liked it very, very much.

****

I was awash in sensations. Bobby's breathing was as clear to me as if it were my own. The scent of him filled my nose as it followed my lips along his skin. I felt every part of him as I slid my body along his.

Bobby stopped kissing me for a moment, and I took the opportunity to bury my face in his neck. He was below me on the bed, around me, inside me. And I needed a minute. I couldn't look into his sky blue eyes just then.

Because I was having an epiphany.

As a child, when I believed in fairy tales, I thought that people fell in love slowly. You went on three dates, then you had sex, then you started to like each other a little more and spend all your time together, then you fell in love, then you got married.

But I quit believing in fairy tales when I was still a very young girl, and at eighteen, I quit believing in love altogether. I mean, I believed Candace when she said she loved Jack, or Chelsea when she said she loved Henry. It was written all over them. But I didn't think it could happen to me. Love was this foreign thing that would never be a part of my life.

But there I was, in the throes of passion with my Bobby, and I was absolutely certain I'd fallen love with him. My head spun, my stomach churned. It reminded me of the sensation I experienced after getting off a carnival ride. I felt like my life was being ripped apart while simultaneously basking in the glow of a strange sense of comfort and rightness.

The worst part was it was completely out of my control. I couldn't stop it or slow it down. I couldn't steer it or direct it. I was at the mercy of this thing.

Right in the middle of this sudden and unwanted realization, I had an orgasm. Bobby wouldn't let me not have one. He worked so hard at it. And I was beholden to his desires at that moment. He wanted my body to give up its every sensation to him. So it did. I couldn't do anything about it.

I screamed out his name, and he answered in a guttural roar as we climaxed together. I looked into his eyes as he pulled back and watched what he'd done, what we'd done.

And I loved him even more.

Not till afterward, when he pulled me tightly against his chest, my back to him, his arms enveloping me like a warm, strong blanket, his breathing deep and even near my ear, was I able to think again.

What I felt for Bobby changed nothing. Because Hayden Morrison still needed a wife. And I couldn't be Hayden's wife.

I could absolutely see myself with Bobby. Maybe if he'd been a school teacher or a bus driver, or maybe a graphic designer. We'd fall asleep like this every night, me wrapped in his arms. I'd wake up to him every morning. We'd fight. We'd play. I would be happy.

But I could not be hostess to businessmen in a mansion. I could not take up tennis and hang out at the country club. I couldn't be what Hayden Morrison needed to fulfill his role.

So this was all doomed to come to an end. I would always have the memories of Bobby and me. That's what I would cling to when I watched him marry someone else, when I watched him grow a family, while I remained alone.

I would be alone because now I knew what it was to love someone—no, now I knew what it was to love *him*—I wouldn't be able to pretend with anyone else. I wouldn't be able to go through the motions.

I lay there in bed, Bobby asleep at my side, tears streaming quietly down my face, and I grieved.

Chapter 15

Yesterday

He didn't look like your average deliveryman. He was wearing a suit and carrying one very small bag.

"This is for Mr. Morrison," he said, holding the bag up by its dainty rope handles.

Smithson Jewelers was printed plainly on the side, along with their triple ring logo.

"He's in a meeting. I can take it." I stretched out my hand.

The man pulled the bag out of my reach. "I am supposed to give it to Mr. Morrison only."

"Well, I'm his assistant, and Mr. Morrison will be unavailable for a least a few more hours." That wasn't exactly true. In fact, I expected Hayden back pretty soon.

The guy chewed on his lip, his wheels turning.

"Mr. Morrison trusts me with his life. Ask anyone," I said. That was a very true statement. Although I doubted Hayden wanted me to see what was in that bag.

"Fine. Sign here," the guy said, shoving an old-fashioned clipboard beneath my nose. "And print your name above the signature. This is very expensive. If it goes missing, I want to know who to blame."

I did as he asked without giving him the dirty look

he deserved. He handed over the bag and left.

My stomach in knots, I took the bag into Hayden's office and locked the door behind me. I sat down at his desk and placed the package in front of me gingerly, like it was a bomb about to explode. And in a way, I knew it was.

I only stared at the bag for about five minutes before I dipped my hand inside and pulled out the small velvet box. I had completely stopped breathing by the time I pulled the box open and peered inside.

Nestled in the velvet folds sat the most perfect thing I'd ever seen. Instead of one large, garish diamond, five miniscule ones sparkled around a white gold band, which itself looped around in an elegant display of curves and intertwining ropes.

I knew what it meant. It meant Bobby wanted me as much as I wanted him. It meant Bobby knew me better than anyone else on this planet. It meant Bobby and I were through.

****

I was still sitting at his desk when he came back. I hadn't bothered to unlock the door or move from his chair. The lock clicked as he used his key. He walked in, handsome and perfect, and heartbreakingly sexy.

He took in the scene: me sitting at his desk, still and terrified, the abandoned bag lying on the desk, and the ring box, still opened, in front of me. He stopped a few feet away and just stood there for a moment. Slowly, he approached, setting the folders he held in the crook of one arm down gently, all the while his eyes locked on me.

"I was supposed to have more time to talk you into it before I actually gave that to you," he said. His tone was casual, but his body was tight and tense.

I didn't say anything. All the words I'd practiced stayed bottled up inside me as I looked into those ocean blue eyes.

"I…uh…I think the good news is I'm ready to write that check for the finder's fee. After all, you did find me the woman I want to marry." He tried for light and humorous. It didn't work.

I stood. My legs were shaking as I walked around the desk. "Bobby…"

He held up his hand. "Before you say anything, let me do the thing where I tell you why."

I shook my head, a tear escaped the corner of my eye and flew into my hair.

His voice was soft, aching. He already knew where this was headed. "It's a pretty good speech."

"I can't," I choked out.

"Meg."

I shook my head again. "I made a call while you were gone."

It had been the one thing I was able to do after finding that ring. Because I knew I would hurt him. And I never wanted that. So to ease the sting I'd called the one person I'd been avoiding.

"You see," I told him, my voice gaining strength. "There's this woman. She's perfect for you. Absolutely perfect in every way. I've known for a while now she was the one I needed to set you up with. But I didn't because…because I wanted more time," I admitted. "But tonight…tonight you're going out with her. The arrangements are all made."

Keeping a wide berth around him, I made my way to the door. Bobby didn't say anything, he just followed my movements with his eyes.

"I will put it all in your calendar. I'll see you at the restaurant tonight," I said quickly as I pulled open the door and escaped.

As soon as I was free of his gaze, I ran into the women's restroom and had a complete meltdown in the back stall.

****

I looked at Amber and thought again how perfect she was for Hayden. Grace's younger sister was every bit as gorgeous as Grace but far more refined. Where Grace was loud and rough, Amber was soft and smooth.

With an upbringing similar to Hayden's and a business degree, Amber fit into the Morrison family like a glove. She was ambitious but not overly concerned about having a great career of her own. She'd confessed to me that she would work hard until the day she got pregnant, then she planned to stay home with the kids. She was also smart, funny, and into bodybuilding. Yes, I'd actually found a woman with the same bizarre-ass hobby as Hayden. And she was smoking hot as a result.

I tried desperately not to feel inadequate sitting beside her. But it was impossible. Soon, the man I loved would be with this woman, admiring her, touching her, making love to her.

I shook off the thought. "So, you said you haven't met Hayden before."

She shook her head. "Never had the chance."

Amber had been across the country for college and had only moved back home recently. And while her sister was tight with Hayden's sister-in-law, that hadn't translated into an introduction at any point.

"I am so confident this will work out, I'm already planning the engagement party."

Amber laughed and rested her hand on her chin. "Is that right?"

I nodded.

"I wonder…" she said, a sparkle in her eye.

"What?"

"Well, we've been sitting here for the last twenty minutes." She gestured to the intimate little booth we'd acquired at the restaurant. "And you've been telling me all about Hayden."

"Yeah, that was the plan. Meet here early to talk about him before he arrives." I didn't know what the hell she was getting at.

She smiled. "I think *you* have a thing for him."

I did briefly think about pretending to be appalled. I could hear myself in my head. "Me? What?! No way! That's ridiculous." But I couldn't do it. "Yeah, maybe I do. He's all the things I told you he is and he's insanely hot, as you will see soon. But that's not relevant."

"Not relevant?" Her eyebrows shot up.

"It's not. I'm not his type. He's not mine. Hayden and I aren't a thing. It's not a thing. But you and him, you guys will be great together."

"This is straight-up bizarre. You are setting me up with a guy you are—"

"I have a little crush on." I interrupted her with a half-truth to keep her from saying more. "So what?"

She stared at me. Fortunately, we didn't have time to get into it any further because Hayden stormed into the restaurant like a gorgeous hurricane. He spotted me right away and headed toward us, his gaze locked on mine.

I felt a little like a kid in trouble. I hadn't seen Hayden since I'd walked out of his office that afternoon. The look on his face was that of an angry parent dealing with a contentious child.

When he reached the table, his gaze shifted to Amber and his features softened. He smiled brightly at her. They greeted each other, shaking hands and making nice.

I sat in the corner of the booth beside Amber while Hayden sat directly across from her, leaned forward, attention her way, completely ignoring me.

We ordered a full meal at my suggestion. I knew they'd get along so well and have so many things to talk about there was no need to ease into it from a shorter "just drinks" kind of date.

Throughout the meal, Hayden and Amber talked animatedly. They discussed everything they had in common. They talked about their families and the people they both knew. They went on about business school. They chatted about bodybuilding.

"Hey," Hayden said, leaning back in the booth. I knew from eating with him a million times it was a sign that he was full. "Are you going to Fitness Festival tomorrow?"

"You know," Amber said. "This is the first year I've been in town for it, and I completely forgot to get tickets."

"I've got two. You want to go?"

Amber's face lit up like a freaking Christmas tree. "Absolutely."

All through dinner, my irritation had been my constant companion. It sat on my shoulders reminding me all of this was my fault. The better they got along, the more Hayden smiled at her, the more pissed off I became. Now they'd made a second date already. Barely an hour had passed since they'd met!

"What's Fitness Festival?" I asked, jumping in for the first time.

Hayden's eyes slid to me. Rather than angry, he looked spiteful now. It was a little scary. "It's an annual conference where workout freaks like Amber and I go to learn about the newest techniques and products. They always have special guest speakers and performers. It's not something you would be interested in."

Fire burned in my belly, and I had no doubt it showed on my face. I hadn't missed the way he'd purposely left me out, pitting him and her against the slackers like me.

"What do you know about what interests me?" I shot back.

Hayden folded his arms across his chest. "A whole hell of a lot, Meg. A whole hell of a lot." Then he turned to Amber, and that softness returned. He smiled. "Meg likes art and hanging out at the beach. She's fascinated with fish, especially big ones, and tiny birds. She loves to yell at complete strangers at ball games. It may be her favorite part of the game, in fact. And she wants to be into yoga, but she doesn't think she's coordinated enough to do it well. You know what she *isn't* interested in?" he asked her, hooking his thumb my way. "She *isn't* interested in me."

I was torn between being so angry I could jump up on the seat and clobber him in the head and being completely intrigued by how Amber would respond to his tirade.

"Hmmm," Amber said, leaning back in her own

seat and imitating him. She had the strangest look on her face, and her gaze remained focused on Hayden. "I'm not sure I buy that."

"No?" he asked, his head cocked to one side like a curious puppy.

"No. See, before you got here, she talked about you. In fact, she wouldn't shut up about you," Amber told him.

"That's because I was prepping you to meet him!" I practically yelled. My elevated tone gathered the attention of several people nearby. I lowered my voice. "It's a perfectly normal thing to do. I *am* his matchmaker."

They both completely ignored me.

"Oh yeah, what did she say about me?" Hayden asked.

It was insane. It was as if I wasn't there!

"She told me how smart and funny you are. That you have these responsibilities and you're good at fulfilling them, but deep down you love to have fun, too. She says you're kind, but you don't want everyone to know that. And…" She paused for dramatic effect. "She thinks you're hot."

Hayden grinned. "Is that right?"

I lost it, completely lost my shit right there in the restaurant. "Okay, that's it! Let me out," I demanded.

Amber did as she was told, and I shuffled out of the booth. Neither of them spoke to me, and I didn't have anything to say. I just walked out of the restaurant and out to the curb to catch a cab.

****

It was hard being an asshole. It took a lot of work. And while some people were capable of doing it

167

without looking back or feeling any regret, I was not one of those people.

I felt horrible about my behavior the minute my butt hit the seat of that cab. Then I'd gone home and wallowed in it for another thirty minutes before calling Amber to apologize.

She'd been just leaving the restaurant when I called. She wasn't angry with me. In fact, she apologized for teasing me. I assured her that she'd done nothing wrong and asked if she and Hayden were still going to the conference together. Her confirmation that the date was still on nearly killed me. But I gushed about how happy that made me before hanging up.

It didn't take long after that to decide to call a ride share and head to Bobby's place.

"Hi," he said, taking in my appearance outside the elevator with a smile I didn't deserve.

"Um…Can I come in?"

"Always." He stepped aside and gestured for me to move into the apartment.

I walked into the living room, threw my purse on the couch, and turned to him. "I'm sorry," I said simply.

"I'm happy to see you," he told me, as if I hadn't just apologized for being a horrible asshole.

"I don't know why. I suck."

He moved toward me and put his hands on my waist. "Can we just call this what it is? You and I, neither of us want to be with anyone else. And neither of us want to see the other one with anyone else."

I nodded. "That's the truth. But it doesn't change the situation."

He sighed. "Okay. Then can we just not talk about it for a minute? Can we just go to bed, make love, and cuddle?"

I couldn't think of anything I wanted more.

Chapter 16

Seven hours ago

"What are we going to do?" I asked.

Bobby was still coming down after our morning sex session, and he frowned at me.

"I mean it." I propped myself up on my elbow to get a better look at him. "This can't go on. We have to stop this. You have to move on. You have a freaking date today."

"What about you?" he asked.

"What about me?"

"Aren't you going to move on?"

Damn. I didn't lie to Bobby. Honesty was our thing. How could I tell him how I felt about this?

"Not right now," I said softly.

"Why don't I get the same courtesy?" he asked.

"What?"

"You get time to get over us. Did it ever occur to you I might need time to get over us, too?"

I looked into his eyes, and for the first time since I'd realized I loved him, I stopped being so self-absorbed, I couldn't see past my own nose.

"Do you love me?" I asked him.

"Yes."

My stomach flipped completely over, and my heart stuttered. "But you know why we can't be together, right?"

He looked away from me and ran his hand through his hair. "Yeah, I know." He sat up in the bed. "You wanna get breakfast? You must be hungry. You hardly touched your dinner last night."

"I didn't think you were paying attention to me at all last night."

He swung his feet over the side of the bed. "I'm always paying attention to you, Meg."

****

"Where are we going?" I asked, as Bobby took another turn.

"A little post-breakfast adventure. You have time, don't you?"

I shrugged. I wasn't about to end my day with Bobby if I could help it. Because after he dropped me off, he would be headed to meet Amber at the fitness convention thing. And I was jealous as hell about it.

He pulled into an underground parking garage and stopped in an aisle. As soon as we exited the car, a man in a uniform approached, greeted us, and took his keys. Then we headed up on an elevator.

"Where are we?" I asked.

"The Baldy Building. Have you heard of it?"

Everybody at Morrison knew the legend of the Baldy Building. It was still talked about occasionally in the lunchroom and after meetings. Seven years ago, Hayden and Jack had an historic battle over this building. A beautiful, old apartment high-rise in the SOMA district, Hayden had wanted to tear it down to build expensive condos. But after an epic war, Jack won the day, and instead Morrison and Sons restored the building to its former glory and rented it out at reasonable rates.

"There's an empty unit," Bobby said casually as the elevator took us to the top floor.

"How is that possible?" I asked. The place was in high demand, with a waiting list spanning decades, not years.

"I set it aside." He turned to me and winked. "You can do that when you're the boss."

The elevator doors opened, and he ushered me out into the hallway. Only one door greeted us up here, directly across from the elevator. But I knew there were four units per floor in this building. Each held two two-bedroom apartments, one one-bedroom apartment, and one three-bedroom apartment.

I was confused, so as Bobby worked on the lock I asked, "Why is there only one unit up here?"

"This one was created for the owner. It takes up the entire top floor. It has four bedrooms, three baths, an open-style den, and a private rooftop garden. And there's one other special feature. Here. I'll show you." He swung the door open and ushered me inside.

In addition to being completely empty, the apartment was clean and freshly painted. The hardwood floors had been recently scrubbed and shone in the morning light spilling through the large windows.

Bobby walked to the center of the massive living room. "The tenants just moved out last week. My staff are pretty amazing, right?" Bobby never passed up an opportunity to praise his staff. It was one of the many things I loved about him.

"Yeah, it looks great," I said in awe.

The room held a cozy fireplace, built-in shelving, and tall windows with a killer view. Bobby pushed open a set of old-fashioned wooden swinging doors to show me the large and recently renovated kitchen. Then he took my hand and ushered me toward the other side of the living room. The den stood guard at the head of a short hallway which led to bedrooms and bathrooms. None of the rooms were huge, like in Bobby's place, but each was large enough for its purposes. The whole thing made me feel warm and happy.

After seeing the bedrooms, Bobby pulled me to the very end of the hallway rather than going back toward the living room as I expected. There, a door with one of those push bars, like an emergency exit, waited for us. Hayden propped it open, and we walked out onto a lower roof.

He walked across it, pulling me along. Someone had been up there with a rake and hoe recently. A set of raised flower beds overflowed with fresh blooms and a variety of vegetables and herbs. Distracted by the plants, I didn't notice the building that sat on the roof until Bobby pulled me through another door.

It was almost like a cottage. About the size of a single car garage, it perched alone on the roof, surrounded by flower beds. Large windows wrapped all the way around the small building.

"It was originally a garden house," he explained, as we entered the room.

Made of glass and wood, the room was empty with the exception of a sink and vanity tucked into one corner. The smell of fresh wood stain still hung in the air.

"I had the water source put in here recently," Hayden said, nodding toward it.

His hands were shoved into his pockets, his body

stiff. I walked slowly around the room, looking it over. "The light in here is incredible."

He shrugged. "I was thinking it would make a good art studio. That's why I put in the sink…Do you think it's big enough?"

I gazed at the room in wonder. "The view, the light, the space. It's perfect. I dream of a studio like this."

He gave a little grunt, and I peeked over at him. Sadness enveloped him. His eyes fixed on the ground in front of him, he nodded slowly. "Well, thanks for the opinion. I guess I'll offer it that way then, apartment with studio."

"Wait. That doesn't make sense. You were holding this place just to ask me if this room would make a good studio?"

He didn't answer, and he kept his head down. And that's when my dumbass brain caught up to my dumbass heart. I sucked in a deep breath. "Bobby." He didn't raise his head. So I pulled on his arm and yanked his hand out of his pocket so I could hold it. I said again, "Bobby." His eyes met mine and they were pained. "This was supposed to be our place, wasn't it?"

He swallowed hard. "You never let me make my proposal. It was more than the ring, more than a marriage certificate. I wanted to give you the life you always wanted." He pulled his hand out of mine and stepped back. "But I can't do that. Because I'm not *who* you want."

My heart broke all over again. I grieved for a life I thought I couldn't have, only this time it was even clearer. Now I knew Bobby loved me enough to let me stay true to myself. Now I knew we could meet halfway.

He moved away from me, crossing the room, toward the door. I reached out to him, but he continued on his path. "I need to go meet Amber. I don't know why I showed you this." It was a confession, an apology. "I didn't do it to make you feel guilty."

Tears streamed down my cheeks, and his face blurred in my vision. "Why do you think we can't be together?" I asked him. "What did you mean this morning when you said you knew why?"

He paused at the door, half in and half out. He held my gaze. "I know you don't feel the same way about me that I feel about you."

I couldn't breathe.

"I know you like hanging out with me. I know you find me attractive, and even that you're jealous when I go out with other girls. But that's not the same as this." He thumped on his chest. "You can't return it. And there isn't a house or a studio or a goddamn thing I can do about it."

****

Present day

"He left me there, at the Baldy Building, in that beautiful studio, just steps from that beautiful apartment. I walked through it, imagining how it would look with our things in it. I saw my collection of knitted kitchen towels hanging from the cabinets. I saw that stupid pin-up blanket of Bobby's draped over a couch, a new couch, one we'd bought together. And I saw the bedroom, an exact replica of his. I sobbed the whole time. Eventually, I went down to the parking garage. Bobby's car was gone, of course, but the man in uniform approached me right away and put me in a limo. So that's how I got here," I tell Grace and Meno. "I fell in love with Hayden Morrison, then I pushed him away. And now I've wrecked my entire life."

Meno arrived back at the house about twenty minutes into my story. He took a seat opposite Grace and me and just sat there silently, listening. His presence was oddly comforting and helped me work up the courage to tell them all the worst parts of the story.

Grace and Meno both stare at me for a long time. I feel a little like the bearded lady at a freak show. Is it that messed up a story? Of course it is. Who am I kidding? I let the man I love believe I didn't care enough about him to make a commitment to him. I let him walk out the door and go on a date with someone else.

"I'm an idiot," I groan.

"No, you're not," Grace says kindly, rubbing my back.

"I am," I argue. "I pushed Bobby away because I didn't think I could be what he needed. But I never asked him *his* opinion about that. I didn't take his feelings into consideration. I was so scared I didn't measure up, I sabotaged everything." I sat up straighter. "I *can* take care of Bobby. I *can* be what he needs. I look after his career every day. I chased off that Jacob guy. I helped him relax and have fun. I made him happy."

"Of course you did," Grace says.

"And Bobby completely accepted me for who I am. He never once asked me to change."

"No," Grace agrees. "He didn't."

"And then I wrecked it all." I feel defeated.

"There is a solution to this problem, you know,"

Meno says.

I look over at him. He looks very handsome, his arms resting on his thighs as he leans toward me, his dark eyes examining me with curiosity and concern.

"What's that?" Grace and I ask at the same time.

He looks pointedly at Grace before turning to me and saying, "Go after him, of course."

"He's right," Grace says.

"He's on a date with your sister." Guilt strains my voice.

Grace waves her hand at me. "Amber will be all right. She's a tough cookie. Besides, it's not like she's fallen in love with him over one date."

I shrug. "I suppose not. But I feel terrible I set her up with a man that…" I trail off, unable to finish.

"Listen, forget about Amber. Do you want Hayden?" Grace asks.

I nod. "Like you wouldn't believe."

"And are you willing to get over all your hang-ups about him being a rich executive?"

I bite my bottom lip. "I want Bobby."

"And that means you have to take Hayden, too," Grace reminds me.

I nod. "I know."

"Then what the hell are we waiting for?" Meno says. He claps his hands together and stands. "Let's get our asses down to Fitness Festival."

Chapter 17

Hayden
Present day

"So that's the whole story," I say. "She dumped me in our dream house. And here I am."

"With Amber," Henry says.

I fold my hands on my lap and look around at the tiny backstage room we're in. And I know I need to go find Amber soon. She's out wandering around Fitness Festival alone.

"We're just friends," I tell my brother-in-law. "We talked after Meg left the restaurant in a huff yesterday. She said she knew Meg had a thing for me, and she wouldn't dream of getting in the middle of our mess. But she's a cool chick, and we became fast friends."

Across the table from me, Hank Tolk looks thoughtful. He finishes his can of soda and leans back, regarding me like a subject of study. "Why'd you run?" he asks.

"Excuse me? I didn't run. *She* did," I protest.

"Doesn't sound like it to me. There you were, in the apartment, wearing your heart on your sleeve, and before she could really respond, you took off." The rock star points at me in accusation.

"She doesn't want me. I can't change that."

"Then why did you take her there?" Henry asks.

I take a deep breath. I hadn't really been sure at the time. But now that I've told the story to Henry and his uncle, I feel I have a better grasp on it. "I guess I was still hoping to change her mind. But then we went there, and I could see how badly she wanted that apartment and studio, and I realized I didn't want to talk her into being with me. I wanted her to want me the way I want her. I wanted her to love me the way I love her."

This is so hard to admit. But I am in it now. I've just told them the entire story. I don't see any reason to hold back.

"Maybe she does. Maybe now you'll never know," Hank says.

"I think I'm starting to hate your uncle," I tell Henry.

He laughs and exchanges a glance with Hank. "He's a real pain in the ass all right."

My phone buzzes in my pocket, and I look down at it. "That's Amber," I tell them after reading the text message. "She's looking for me."

Henry stands. "Tell her to meet you by the Pilates studio."

To my surprise, Hank stands, too. "You're coming?" I ask him.

"Sure. I want to see what this Amber has to say about your love life." He grins.

We walk out together, and make our way through the thick, black curtain that separates the backstage area from the public area. Amber is standing just to the left of a full-blown Pilates class taking place right there in the middle of the convention.

Fortunately, she sees me, because there is no way she'd hear me over the din of the instructor shouting instructions into her microphone. Amber makes her way over, her face growing more and more excited as she sees my companions.

"Hey," I say, when she gets close enough to hear me over the "One and two and three more!" of the instructor nearby.

"Oh my God! Hi," she says, her eyes flitting between me and the legendary rock star standing to my right.

"Amber, this is Chelsea's husband, Henry, and his uncle Hank," I say.

"Wow. Hi."

"So Amber. Tell me. Do you think Meg is in love with Hayden?" Hank asks.

"Way to ease into that," I complain.

He ignores me, and so does Amber. She's so excited he's talking to her, I may as well not even be there. She nods vigorously. "Oh, definitely."

"Uncle Hank," Henry says. "You've been made. We should get out of here."

We all look up to see several people making a beeline for us.

"Yeah. You'd better go before you ruin the surprise." I turn to them. "Hey, thanks for listening."

"No problem." Hank fist-bumps me. "I hope it all works out, man."

"Stay for the show," Henry calls, as he turns to follow.

Amber and I watch as Henry ushers his uncle back behind the black curtain. Then she turns to me and throws her arms around me. "Oh my God! I just met Hank Tolk!" she squeals.

I hug her back and tell her, "If we hang around for

another hour, we can watch him perform. And I'm pretty sure I can get my brother-in-law to get us the best view of the stage."

I need a distraction tonight to keep me from running back to Meg without thinking it through. To keep me from ripping my heart to shreds all over again.

"You are the best!" she says as she kisses my check.

I lift her up so her feet leave the floor. "I'm glad you think so." I set her down and she moves far enough away to look at me. "Really, it's just because my sister married well."

"Hayden. Hayden Robert Morrison."

I turn my head instinctively at the sound of my name coming through a speaker somewhere. Swiveling toward the noise, I focus on the area where the Pilates instructor had just been. Only it isn't the lithe blonde holding the headset and speaking into it, now. She's a few feet away, grinning at the woman who is calling my name, staring straight at me, my nemesis, my heartbreak, the love of my life.

"I…I want to ask you something," Meg stutters into the microphone. I can barely comprehend what is happening when she says, "Marry me, Bobby." She says it quickly, on a hard breath.

I cannot seem to wrap my head around what is going on. Meg is standing a couple dozen feet away from me, looking like she's just seen a ghost. Her face is drained of color, her eyes swimming with tears and rimmed in red. But she's here, at Fitness Festival, proposing to me over a microphone in front of hundreds of work-out freaks, Grace and Meno, who've appeared out of nowhere, Grace's sister, and having re-emerged from the black curtain, my brother-in-law, and one rock star.

Then she's handing the microphone over to the Pilates instructor and running through the crowd. She weaves through men and women perched on mats, half in and half out of Pilates poses, their mouths hung open, their eyes wide as they watch her.

I take up the chase as she bolts past a booth selling the latest high-protein powder and nearly knocks over a woman handing out samples of energy bars. The path clears up after that, and Meg really puts on the speed as she makes her way toward the front door.

I am fast. Faster than Meg. All that working out has to count for something, not to mention my significantly longer legs. I catch up to her right after she bursts through the swinging glass doors and launches herself toward the sidewalk.

I throw my arms around her from behind and haul her to my chest. "Hey there, speedy. Calm down a minute," I say, my voice low.

Meg is definitely sobbing. Her breath stutters with great gulps of air, and her body trembles. So I turn her to the side and pick her up. She immediately buries her head in my chest as I walk around to the parking garage and make my way to the car.

I am moving slower with Meg in my arms, being more cautious with my precious cargo. Both Meno and Grace catch up to me, as does Henry.

"We're okay," I tell them. "Henry, make sure Amber gets home from the show all right."

They don't argue, or say anything more. They just fade away. Meg is calmer by the time I get her into my car. But she's switched from burying her face in my chest to burying her face in her hands.

I walk around to the driver's side and get in. I pull the car out onto the road before asking her, "Where do you want me to take you?"

"Your place," she says quietly.

"Really?" I ask. "I thought you hated my place?"

She shakes her head. "No. I don't. I mean, I did." She wipes at her face and stares out the window. "But then I found all the little things that make it yours, that reflect you."

"Like my frat-boy pictures?" I tease.

"I looked at them closer. They're of you and your friends and your family. You keep the people you care about right on your wall. That's pretty freaking amazing."

"Hmmm. What else?"

"That stupid blanket on your couch. Jack gave it to you. God knows why. The thing is ugly as sin. But he did. I know because he told me. And you kept it. And then there's the box on your nightstand that has your grandfather's broken watch in it, and the painting...Bobby, the painting. I want to go to your place."

"Okay," I say simply, making a turn that will take us to my building.

We sit in silence for a while. Then I feel her hand on my upper arm. I pull my own hand off the steering wheel and take hers in mine.

She squeezes. "I kind of panicked when I saw you with Amber. I came there to talk and...I saw you two together. You looked so happy..."

"She'd just met Henry's uncle, and apparently she's a big fan. I told her we'd see his show. That's why she was hugging me," I explain.

Meg is silent.

"See, Henry's uncle is like the special guest star at the convention and he—"

"*You* looked happy, too."

"I was just hanging out with my friend. Believe me, Meg, every minute without you is torture."

We are silent again, and we stay that way, hand in hand, riding through the city, until we reach my building. I pull into my parking spot, and we both unbuckle our seatbelts before shifting to face one another.

"Why did you come to the convention this afternoon?" I ask gently.

She toys with the palm of my hand, running her fingers over it. "I came to tell you I love you. See, I think maybe you were unaware of how I felt. And that's my fault. Because from the minute I realized you are…you are *it* for me…I tried to keep it from you. And that was so wrong. Because you and I, we don't keep things from each other."

I feel as though, for the first time in days, I can breathe.

"Why did you turn me down yesterday?" I ask her.

She swallows hard and meets my gaze. "I didn't want to be a corporate wife. And I didn't think I *could* be…I'm still a little shaky on it, to be honest…The bottom line is, I thought I wasn't what you needed…"

My chest tightens again. I'm on such a roller coaster, I wouldn't be surprised if I had a heart attack any minute now. "And?" I prompt.

"So I tore my own heart out to do what I thought was best for you. And then this morning…This morning, you offer me…everything. You *and* the life I want for myself." A tear slips down her cheek. "It's more than I would have ever known to ask for. And then I blew it."

I wipe the tear from her face with my thumb. "Baby, you can always have me. That's a given. I'm yours. You're my matchmaker, and you handpicked the perfect woman, just for me." I lean toward her. "I love you, Chuck."

She attacks. It isn't just the deep kiss. It's all of her. She crawls right up on my lap, wedging herself between me and the steering wheel, her legs straddling my hips.

I am almost ready to forget where I am and pull her skirt up when she pulls back. "Shit. We have to get up that elevator."

I chuckle. "Yes, sweetheart, we do."

"Bobby?"

"Hmmm?"

"I am completely, insanely in love with you."

I point at the security camera attached to the ceiling of the garage. "Baby, get out of the car before this turns into something seedy that gets spread on the Internet."

****

"So, I think we should replicate this room exactly in the new place," Meg tells me, her hand drifting slowly up and down my chest.

I am lying on my back, looking up at the ceiling and trying to catch my breath after she blew me away. She is propped up on her elbow, her perfect body pressed against my side.

"Well, sweetheart, I hate to break it to you, but that place in the Baldy building, the master bedroom is about half the size of this one."

"No worries. I can make it happen. I'm good with space."

I kiss the top of her head. "You're good with everything."

"You wanna get married before we move into the new place?"

I roll over on my side, so we face each other. "We don't have to get married."

"Wait a minute. I humiliated myself this afternoon in front of hundreds of muscle-bound men and women to propose, and you aren't accepting?"

"No. That's not what I'm saying. I'm saying, I don't want you to feel pressured. It's not important that we actually get married."

"You bought the ring," she points out. "That tells me you want to get married."

"I bought the ring for you. You can have it whether you marry me or not. I just want to be with you." I kiss her gently on the nose.

"No. I don't get the ring until we set a date for an actual wedding. And by the way, it will be a Vegas-style elopement."

I chuckle. "Okay. But it doesn't have to be now."

She nods, and I know we're in agreement about this. I would take her as my bride in a heartbeat, but I won't risk scaring her away again. We will do this on *her* timeline.

She plays with my hair for a minute. "Are you going to cut your hair?"

"Do you want me to?"

"No. I don't. I think you're growing it long."

"I was thinking about it."

"That would be very un-CEO-like," she says.

"Yes, it would. But I think I'll do it anyway. Just like I will live in sin with a crazy artist. My job doesn't define me."

She smiles. "No, it doesn't. I suppose the same goes for me, right?"

"I suppose that's true."

"I can be an artist and still live with a rich man."

"Yep. In fact, I'm pretty sure if you let me get us that fancy apartment and buy you a car, you won't even lose your artist's card."

"You wanna buy me a car?"

"Of course. Shit, baby. I want to buy you everything. Everything that you need to be safe and happy."

"You want to take care of me."

"Is that wrong?" I ask, suddenly feeling like maybe I've made a misstep.

"No," she says softly. "It's not wrong. I think I'll let you."

Chapter 18

Three weeks later

Meg smiles at me from across the room, and I think how completely unfair it is that we are separated by so much space and so many people. But she is helping Candace get ready to make the big reveal, and I am standing beside my brother distracting him.

"I can't believe you and Meg moved in together," my mother says.

"Why not, Mom? You didn't complain when Jack and Candace moved in together, or Chelsea and Henry," I say, feeling a little picked on. Meg and I literally just moved into our Baldy Building apartment this morning.

"That's not what I mean," she says, throwing her hand at me. "I mean we just found out you two were dating a few weeks ago. It seems kind of fast."

"Unless…" Jack says, raising his eyebrows. And I remember that conversation we had at Lake Merritt.

"Yeah," I tell him. "It was Meg all along." I glance over at her again. She's laughing at something Candace is saying. Her head is thrown back, and she looks amazing. "She's always been the one," I say softly, more to myself than to them.

"So it's going well? With you and the talented artist?" my dad asks.

"Very well." I can't stop my massive grin. "Except now I have to find a new secretary."

"I like her," my dad says. "She seems like a good catch."

"Hopefully she can put up with you." Jack slaps my back lightly.

I look at him and smirk. "I think I'll do all right. After all, I'm just a boring CEO who has to try to keep the interest of an artist. You're a jailbird who's in love with a lawyer," I say, referring to Jack's multiple stints in local lock-ups because of protests he participated in.

"Then we'll have to help each other keep our women." He throws an arm over my shoulder. "Otherwise we'll end up old and lonely in a nursing home together."

"Fighting until your dying days, no doubt," my mother quips.

Jack and I both laugh at that. We haven't fought in years, but we obviously scarred our mother for life with all the bickering we did in our youth.

"By the way, this is a hell of a birthday party, and I understand that you and Meg are to blame. Thank you," Jack says.

"We had fun planning it. I'm glad you liked it." I look around the ballroom we'd rented for the occasion. The party is winding down now. About a hundred guests came and went over the course of the night. The food is nearly gone, the free drinks well imbibed upon, and the massive cake has a pretty big dent in it. "I think your wife is ready to go home, Jack." I point to Candace, who is walking toward us with Chelsea, who has Sandy perched on her hip and Meg at her heels.

"Hi, babe," he says, as she approaches.

"I have one more present for you," she tells him, holding out a small box.

Jack has been heavily embarrassed by the presents, especially since he tries to live a pretty humble life fighting for the rights of the disadvantaged. That's why I got him this party instead of a material thing. I think he appreciates that.

His face screws up as he stares dispassionately at the box. "I really don't need anything else."

"Then consider it a gift for Sandy," she says sweetly.

"Okay," he agrees reluctantly, a confused look on his face. He knows he can't argue now, because Jack would do anything for his daughter.

We all watch as Jack opens the box to reveal a set of car keys. "You bought me a car?"

"I did," Candace says, nodding. "And the car seat is already installed. And I gave your car away to one of those charities that fixes up old cars and gives them to families in need."

He stares at her, his mouth dropped open.

"Don't worry, Jack. I've seen it, and it's a pretty ugly car. Candace wouldn't embarrass you with a fancy car." This time I slap him on the back. "Take your wife home."

After we've said our goodbyes to Jack and Candace and everyone else is making their way out, I pull Meg aside and take her to the office.

Beatrice greets us with a smile. "How did it go?"

"Great." My smile is practically permanent at this point. "Do you have a bill ready? We'd like to pay it before we leave."

"Of course." She turns to her computer and begins

clicking away.

While Beatrice works on preparing the bill, Meg stands beside me, running her thumb obsessively over the credit card in her hand.

"You're going to rub the numbers off," I say, amused. She bites her lip and leans into me. I caress her shoulder. "You can do this, baby," I say quietly.

Meg is holding a credit card with her name on it, but it's on my credit line and I pay the bill. She hasn't used it for anything yet. And she's having trouble taking that first step. So I suggested she use it to pay for Jack's party. Since it is something I planned to pay for anyway, it seems like a good way to ease her into it.

Beatrice hands us the bill, and Meg hands her the card. After she signs, we thank Beatrice and ask her to send our regards to her staff for a job well done. Then Meg and I make our way out to the parking lot.

The last of the people from the party are wandering around the lot as well, and we call out to a few of them before ducking into the hybrid I bought her last week. Only when we're in the car do we finally talk about it.

"That wasn't so bad, was it?" I ask, taking her hand and interlacing our fingers.

She lets out a breath, as if she's been holding it this entire time. "It's a lot to adjust to in a short time, you know. The apartment, the car, and now this credit card."

"I know." I also know I should probably slow things down to make it easier on her, but I can't seem to do that. "It's like that for me, too."

She looks at me, her head cocked. "How's that?"

"I was unhappy for a long time, Chuck. From the day my dad told me I would inherit the company to the day you walked into my office, I lived on pins and needles. My closest companion was self-doubt, just like yours was self-sufficiency. And now, I have you. I am happy and relaxed. You keep me satisfied in my personal life, and you believe in me and give me strength in my professional life. I am so full now because of you."

She leans over and kisses me gently. "Damn, you have a way with words, Bobby. Take me home, to *our* home, and I'll let you take care of me. And"—she grins— "I'll take care of you, too."

****

Fourteen months later

"So what are the chances she'll even remember this?" I ask Jack, just to be a pain in the ass.

"What, you don't remember your second birthday party? I do."

"Yeah, well, you were almost five when I turned two."

"She's having fun," Jack says, gesturing to my niece.

I have to admit Sandy does look like she's having fun. She's wearing a Wonder Woman costume that Meg bought her, a princess tiara, and a pair of pink flip-flops. She is currently dancing around like Snoopy, accompanied by her mother and my girlfriend.

"Aren't there supposed to be like a ton of kids everywhere?" I ask.

"We had the kid party yesterday," he told me. "We had like thirty kids down at the park playing games and stuff. It was fun."

"I can't believe you didn't invite me," I say, in mock offense.

"You'll get invited to the kids' party when Meg pops one out."

I laugh. "Some day."

"Really? You've talked about it?"

I nod. "Sure."

"And you both want kids?"

"Yes. We want exactly two. Meg doesn't want to have an only child who will grow up lonely like she did, and I don't want to have a middle child."

Jack elbows me in the ribs. "Yeah. I'm playing the world's smallest violin for you over here, Hayden."

I chuckle.

"The poor middle child in this family is the CEO of a thriving, growing business, has a beautiful, talented girlfriend, a proud father, and the world at his feet."

"If only I could settle this secretary situation," I complain.

"Still can't find a good one?"

"That's not the problem. Tessa is a fantastic assistant. But I can't convince Meg to stop coming in to my office nearly every day to harass her."

"Well, maybe if your newest secretary wasn't a gorgeous twenty-five-year-old it wouldn't be such a problem," he quipped.

Initially, when Meg and I became an open couple, she'd interviewed and hired my new secretary. Then, when that one didn't work out, she'd hired the next one. After going through four, I took it upon myself to find my own assistant.

The problem was that Meg was looking for two things, perfection—which was impossible for these poor people to achieve—and homeliness, or at least age, or in one case, gender.

But none of them were what *I* needed. What I really needed was someone like Meg. And Tessa was close. Though no one could live up to Meg, she was busy being a successful artist by day and keeping me happy in the evenings, so if I needed to replace her, Tessa was a good fit.

Apparently, however, Meg was jealous. And as much as I knew I needed to put a stop to it, for Tessa's sake, I couldn't help but feel loved and wanted when Meg came by the office to "check on things."

"Tessa knows her stuff. Eventually, Meg will come around," I tell him.

"She's crazy about you," Jack says.

The woman in question turns her head and catches my eye. Her smile is radiant. She spins around and winks over her shoulder in a flirty move.

"I know. I am one lucky son of a bitch," I tell him.

We stand there for a while, watching our three women dance around to Disney tunes in the middle of our childhood backyard on a beautiful Sunday afternoon. Later, Meg and I will go hang out with Sonya. Then we'll go home and probably eat dinner and cuddle up on the couch to watch the next episode of our current show.

We'll go to sleep, her wrapped in my arms, and me more content that I'd ever been in all the years leading up to the day Meg walked into my life.

"Hey," Meg says, pulling me out of my daydream as she walks up to us. She wraps her arms around my neck and runs her hands over my long hair, which is currently tied back in a modest ponytail. Meg loves the long-haired CEO look.

"I need to talk to you," she says, backing up and

taking me by the hand.

"Guess I'm in trouble. Talk to you later, Jack." I follow her to the far side of the pool, away from my family.

She stops and turns to me, taking both my hands in hers. "I love you," she says. She tells me this all the time now. But I never get tired of hearing it.

"I love you, too."

"I decided something recently and thought it was time to share it with you."

"Oh yeah?"

Meg lets go of one of my hands and reaches into the small purse she has flung over her shoulder. "Look," she says, gesturing with her head.

I turn to see my entire family lined up on the other side of the pool, watching us. Even Sandy is still as she gazes at me from the perch of her father's arms.

"I don't under—" I turn back to see Meg on her knees in front of me.

I drop to my own knees on instinct.

"What are you doing? You're supposed to stand up."

I shake my head. "If you're on the ground, then so am I."

Meg laughs. "Okay, Bobby. Have it your way."

I look to see what she's pulled out of her purse. It's the small velvet box that was once delivered by a careless jeweler to my office.

"I see you found your ring."

"You didn't hide it very well," she points out.

No, I hadn't, because I wanted her to have it. "So what are you doing with it now?"

"I thought I'd propose, and then you could put it on

me." She smiles slyly.

I examine her. Her eyes are glowing, her face lit up. And I know she means this. "You're ready?"

"Life with you is so much better than I could ever have imagined," she tells me. "And I don't ever want it to end. I know a piece of paper doesn't change what we have. But I think it will mean something to us both. So, I'm asking you. Will you marry me, Bobby?"

I pluck the box from her fingers and open it. Then I pull out the ring and slip it on her finger before tugging her close to me. "What do you think, Chuck?" I ask, just before kissing her.

A word about the author…

Kay Harris has had a diverse career with jobs ranging from college professor to park ranger. Now she adds author to her repertoire. Kay writes romance novels that contain a little bit of sweet, a dash of sexy, a touch of heartbreak, and a whole lot of fun!

Kay grew up in the Midwest and has since lived all over the western United States including Montana, Wyoming, Utah, Arizona, Nevada, and California. She loves to hike, is obsessed with museums, and enjoys taking her extremely tall and very handsome husband on adventures.

http://kayharrisauthor.com